Blue Eyed

BWWM COWBOY

JAMILA JASPER

WWW.JAMILAJASPERROMANCE.COM

This edition was updated in 2022. The story remains unchanged, but there's a new cover and updated formatting to create a better reading experience.

If you enjoy the story, please remember to leave a review once you're done. 🖤

Sign up to get a text message when my next book drops
https://slkt.io/qMk8

 Created with Vellum

Contents

A PREVIEW

Acknowledgments

Thank you to my most supportive readers:
Christine, Trinity, Monica, Juliette, Letetia,
Margaret, Dash, Maxine, Sheron, Javonda, Pearl,
Kiana, Shyan, Jacklyn, Amy, Julia, Colleen, Natasha,
Yvonne, Brittany, June, Ashleigh, Nene, Nene,
Deborah, Nikki, DeShaunda, Latoya, Shelite, Arlene,
Judith, Mary, Shanida, Rachel,Damzel, Ahnjala,
Kenya, Momo, BJ, Akeshia, Melissa, Tiffany,
Sherbear, Nini, Curtresa, Regina, Ashley, Mia,
Sydney, Sharon, Charlotte, Assiatu, Regina,
Romanda, Catherine, Gaynor, BF, Tasha, Henri, Sara,
skkent, Rosalyn, Danielle, Deborah, Kirsten, Ana,
Taylor, Charlene Louanna, Michelle, Tamika,
Lauren, RoHyde, Natasha, Shekynah, Cassie,
Dreama, Nick, Gennifer, Rayna, Jaleda, Anton,
Kimvodkna, Jatonn, Anoushka, Audrey, Valeria,
Courtney, Donna, Jenetha, Ayana, Kristy, FreyaJo,
Grace, Kisha, Stephanie E., Amber, Denice, Marty,
LaKisha, Latoya, Natasha, Monifa, Alisa, Daveena,
Desiree, Gerry, Kimberly, Stephanie M., Tarah,
Yolanda, Kristy, Gary, Janet, Kathy, Phyllis, Susan

Content Awareness

This is spicy country asf small town romance with a black female lead. This book is around 50,000 words and it's hot, steamy, but not as dark as some of my other titles.

There may be language or situations that make some readers DEEPLY uncomfortable, including strong language in the bedroom.

If you're a bold, open-minded reader who enjoys black woman/white man relationships... welcome to the darker side of interracial romance. 🖤

Prologue

Imani was two years away from completing her PhD. Brian had promised her that when she was finished, they'd finally make their relationship official. They'd have a real wedding with all her jealous, single friends. They'd honey moon in Seoul, South Korea at a luxury city hotel. Then, they'd live in New York and get to work starting a family as soon as possible.

Imani couldn't wait. She loved Brian more than anyone in the world and she was starting to get antsy about weddings and marriage. Many of Imani's older friends from high school were getting married and she was starting to feel like she would never experience the magic of being engaged or the magic of having a wedding.

Imani waited for Brian to get home from work, busying herself so she wouldn't fall into impatience. After her classes, she'd gone to his place to clean up for him and to have dinner ready. Brian worked really hard and he appreciated every little act of kindness Imani did for him. Imani knew that she'd proven to him she was "wife" material. All she had to do was keep this up.

Imani connected her voice recorder's bluetooth to Brian's set of high-powered surround sound speakers. Every opportunity she could, Imani dedicated to studying. She listened to a recording of her earlier lecture that day while she bustled around Brian's place cleaning up after him. First, she dried all of Brian's dishes and put them away. Then, she stuck some white rice in his rice cooker and put some thinly cut chicken breast strips into a pan.

Brian was ascetic in what he ate and he'd insisted that Imani take lessons in Korean cooking a few months earlier so he wouldn't have to "suffer with her greasy food" for the rest of his life. Imani shook her head as she thought of how dramatic Brian could be sometimes. Her Jamaican cooking wasn't greasy at all. Brian just couldn't be bothered to foray into the unfamiliar.

After the kitchen, Imani fussed around Brian's

living room and dining room. His living room was always messy. There were empty mugs with black tea crusted along the sides and bottom. He often left a pair of shoes or two out of place. After cleaning up, Imani worked on running a vacuum over Brian's carpeting.

By the time she'd finished vacuuming her boyfriend's carpet, sweat trickled down her back and across her brow bone. Imani wiped her forehead clean and reminded herself silently, to smile. Cleaning up after Brian wasn't a chore — it was something she did for him, out of love. Women were too reluctantly to go the extra mile these days. It wasn't a trap Imani was going to fall into.

Imani cleaned Brian's bathrooms, using vinegar, bleach and some all-purpose cleaner to scrub every surface to bleached white perfection. She was starting to feel tired, but she was at least satisfied with the job that was being done. Imani couldn't wait until she finished, then she'd take a nice, hot shower, use some of Brian's beauty products from Korea with the labels she couldn't understand and the skin care effects she craved.

First, Imani moved to the final area of hard work — Brian's bedroom. Usually, Brian was neat. He was the kind of guy who swore by self-help books regarding tidiness. When he was stressed, all that Eastern philosophy about "chi" and "feng shui" went out the window, and Brian became a down-right mess.

Since his cousin had been visiting — or so Imani remembered — Brian had been stressed.

She moved onto Brian's bedroom, and began folding clothing, throwing out trash, and stacking books properly onto his bookshelf. A small, balled up piece of cloth on the ground caught Imani's eye. It was small, maybe a sock or something. Except, Brian never wore black socks. Imani bent down and picked it up, lifting it to her eye level.

A thong. A thong that didn't belong to her. Disgusted, Imani dropped the item to the ground. What? She had to have made some kind of mistake. There was no way she'd just found a thong in Brian's bedroom.

Imani ran to his kitchen and found a wooden spoon. She lifted the thong off the ground again and realized that it was exactly what she thought it was. She'd just found women's underwear on the floor of her boyfriend's bedroom.

How could this be possible? The past three nights prior, Brian had asked her not to come over because he had a cousin visiting from Korea. Had that all been a big lie? Imani always thought she'd know what to do if she ever found evidence that her boyfriend had been cheating on her. Faced with reality, her response was much, much different.

She flicked the offending item off the spoon and onto Brian's bed. Imani was in shock. She cleaned the rest of Brian's apartment and continued to cook dinner while contemplating the item she'd just found. Her mind jumped back and forth between believing it to be definitive proof of Brian's infidelity and trying to find some excuse for what she'd found in Brian's bedroom.

Maybe it was his cousin's and it just got stuck to one of his shoes or his t-shirt. Maybe he'd given his cousin his bedroom and moved to the guest room. As Brian got closer and closer to arriving home, Imani grew more frantic. She knew in her heart that what she'd found was a pretty grim condemnation of her boyfriend.

He was cheating on her. He had to be. She'd be foolish to find a thong on her man's floor and believe anything else. Imani tried to figure out what to say, how to say it, but she came up short. By the time Brian arrived at home, she was playing the role of the perfect girlfriend.

"Good evening babe," She said, tiptoeing upwards to kiss Brian on the lips.

"Hey. Is dinner ready?"

"Yup. I made your favorite... Uh... carrot ginger soup and garlic bread."

"Nice."

Brian sat at the dining table and Imani sat across from him. They ate in silence for a while. As they ate, Imani couldn't help but stare at Brian's face. Could it be possible that the man she'd been dating for a full year had been lying to her? If he could lie to her about cheating, was there a chance it had happened before?

"Brian?" Imani asked weakly.

"Yes?"

"Uh... nevermind."

"Listen, the food is fine Imani. I know you've been trying to lose weight for me, right?"

Imani nodded.

That hadn't been it at all. But all of a sudden, she was disarmed by another one of Brian's criticisms. She knew that Brian was trying to help but something about his "help" always made Imani feel like crap. But Brian had to want what was best for her. He'd promised to marry her. He wouldn't go out of his way to make her feel like crap.

Still, Imani couldn't drop the fact that she'd found a thong in his room.

"Brian... While I was cleaning your room, I found a thong."

Brian tilted his head to the side.

"A thong? Must have been Grace's. I slept in the guest room while she was here."

"Oh... Is there a chance I could meet Grace next time she comes?"

Brian shook his head, "I told you... Imani... You're beautiful, but my parents can't find out that I'm dating—."

"I know," Imani finished, "They can't find out that you're dating a black girl."

"Exactly."

Brian continued, "Now you know I love you but we have to wait. Koreans are very traditional."

"Right," Imani said weakly.

The thong she'd found was still weighing on her conscience. Brian had presented a reasonable explanation but something was still off about what he was telling her. Imani hated feeling this suspicious but she wasn't getting the answers and the reassurance from Brian that she craved.

"I want to make love to you tonight," Brian announced after dinner.

"Really?"

Brian nodded.

"Really," He started, "But you know I can't make love to you when you look like this. I want you to be sexy for me. Try to be sexy for me Imani."

"Oh... okay..."

"I have needs Imani, alright? I'm not like other men. I need to be stimulated by a woman. Can you do that?"

Imani nodded and stood up from the dinner table. Brian smiled.

"Come here for a kiss and go change."

She approached Brian and accepted a kiss on the forehead from him. After he kissed her, Imani turned around and walked towards the bedroom. Brian was very kinky by Imani's standards. She had followed his lead in the bedroom but some parts of Brian's desires made her very uncomfortable. Imani just figured if she wanted to get the ring, she'd have to put up with a few oddities here and there.

When Imani slipped away from the table, she had slipped Brian's phone off of it. She knew it was wrong to take his phone, and to spy on him, but she couldn't help herself. She had to know whether he was telling the truth or not and apparently there was only one way for her to find out. Imani's hands were shaking as she stood in the bedroom with her boyfriend's phone.

Brian Choi. The son of a rich Korean millionaire. Graduated from Yale summa cum laude. He was the perfect boyfriend on paper and he had the exact pedigree of the man Imani had hoped to marry. Plus, she was in love with him. Around Brian, Imani always strived to do better. Around Brian, Imani always felt like she was aspiring to something greater.

She unlocked his phone and started scrolling through his text messages. Imani's stomach turned. She didn't have to look long before she started seeing text message after text message. Emily. Trina. Jenny. Imani read as fast as she could. Her fingers lost their grip of his phone and it fell to the ground. She sat on his bed and didn't move a muscle.

Her intuition hadn't been wrong at all. Brian was cheating. He was definitely cheating. Women — not just one woman — had sent him all kinds of provocative photographs and he had replied in kind.

After a few moments, Brian opened the door to his bedroom and looked at Imani on the bed with a look of frustration.

"Imani. I asked you to change," He admonished.

Imani pointed at his phone on the floor.

"Give it up Brian. I know what you've been up to."

"You went through my phone?" Brian asked. His face possessed this wounded look like Imani had just stabbed him.

Imani threw her hands in the air.

"So? So what? Now the problem is I went through your phone and not that I have proof that you cheated on me?"

"It's a serious violation of trust Imani."

Fury overcame Imani and she began to see Brian's insanity for what it was. What on earth was wrong with this guy? He'd cheated on her with over three women and he was trying to make this about his precious "privacy". He had played Imani — and it was clear he didn't feel any remorse for it.

"I swear to God Brian, I will walk out of here right now."

"Walk out? Because you broke my trust, you're going to walk out of here?"

"You're sick!"

"How am I sick Imani?"

"Brian. You cheated on me. How are you not even acknowledging this right now?"

"I think you're really overreacting. Imani, you just need to calm down and we'll discuss this like adults."

"This is not overreacting!" Imani exploded, "This is normal behavior to finding out your boyfriend is a lying bastard. You know what Brian, I'm out of here. Call me when you figure out what you did wrong."

Imani pushed past Brian and collected her stuff. Once Brian saw that she really was going to leave, he began to sing a much different tune.

"You're really leaving?"

"Yes!" Imani called back at him.

"Wait, wait, wait," Brian said, grabbing onto Imani's arm.

She pulled her arm away from him and huffed, "Do not touch me Brian! Do not touch me!"

He pulled away from her and just watched Imani for a moment as she dressed for the weather outside.

"Don't leave Imani..."

She turned around for a final word.

"No. I'm leaving Brian. I don't even know why you're so calm about this, but it's clear, I need to get out of here. This? This is over," Imani said.

She felt tears welling up in her eyes as she turned and left. As Imani made her way home, her sadness started to consume her. She'd been through hard times with Brian before, but cheating? This was a new low, even for him. This was the second time Imani had dumped Brian and she was hoping it would be the last.

Once Imani arrived home, she sat on her bed and cried for a while. Brian. He was so attractive and he'd promised her the exact life she'd been dreaming of. But had it been worth it? Imani knew it would only be self-sabotaging, but she wanted to find out more about the women Brian had cheated with. Women.

"Jesus... I need to listen to myself," Imani whispered under her breath.

After a good, long cry, Imani knew that she couldn't wallow in self-pity any longer. She had important academic work to complete. Imani looked at her phone and called her good friend Franco. He was a few years older than her and worked at the government environmental advocacy agency Imani was hoping to be employed at. She'd met Franco the summer she interned there and he had volunteered to help her with her PhD work.

Since then, they'd become quick friends. Hearing that Imani was utterly distraught, Franco agreed to come over. Imani figured that having company would put her mind at ease and allow her to focus more on her work than on the fact that Brian had cheated on her. Brian was always putting her through something. All of Imani's girl friends were tired of him. Imani had lost her friendship with Kim and with Claire over Brian.

Before Franco arrived, Imani tidied her apartment and changed into a more cozy outfit. At least

Franco didn't care what she was wearing the way Brian did. Imani slipped into cozy fleece-lined black leggings and then an oversized Yale sweatshirt she'd borrowed from Brian a few months back. Imani washed her face and set out a few snacks — carrots and hummus along with some grapes. She knew that Franco was on a health kick and would appreciate a break from tempting delicacies like bagel bites or mini-tacos.

Franco drove up in his red Mazda Protege, dressed in his usual — khakis, a J. Crew button down and a co-ordinating sweater. Franco was trying to quit smoking again, and as he walked up to Imani's apartment , she could see him visibly agitated. At least he'd shaved off his beard. Franco looked much younger without his beard and Imani could see that it definitely improved his self-image.

He knocked on her door and Imani let him in.

"Hey, how are you," Franco said, wrapping Imani up in a big bear hug.

"I feel like shit."

"What happened?"

"I dumped Brian."

"Oh," Franco said flatly.

Imani had a vague idea how Franco felt about Brian, but she had never actually asked him. She was used to so much criticism from her friends that she wasn't interested in hearing more bad news about him.

"What's that tone about?"

Franco sighed, "Well sweetie, it's Brian. The guy who told you to lose ten pounds. The guy who told you that your PhD made him wary of marrying you."

"You don't understand Franco. He's culturally different. That stuff is probably normal back in Korea..."

"Honey, he was born in Virginia," Franco points out. *He's right.*

"Then I don't know. Brian loves me and he wants what's best for me."

"Then why did you dump him then?"

Imani closed her apartment door, realizing that Franco had a good point.

"Well... I found some... girl's underwear on his bedroom floor."

"That bastard!" Franco exclaimed, sitting down and crossing his legs. He looked at Imani like he was trying to squeeze the gossip out of her.

"Listen," Imani continued, noticing Franco's eager expression, "I didn't call you over here to spill all the grimy details. We should probably be studying or working on research."

"Can you give it a rest Imani? For one night? You don't always have to be Miss Perfect. I mean, you just got dumped. When Professor A got divorced, she wore pajamas to class for a month."

Imani chuckled thinking back to that time. Franco had a point. She had stopped to feel her hurt, but only for a moment. It was abnormal to push your feelings so deeply beneath the surface. Franco had a point.

"Fine," Imani sighed, flopping down on the couch next to Franco.

"He cheated on me Franco. I have evidence."

Franco looked at Imani with sympathy in his eyes, but there was no hint of surprise. Why did everyone seem to have a view of Brian that she didn't? Imani was head over heels in love with him, but each time Brian did something egregious, no one around here seemed surprised. It was like they were waiting for her to see something that she just couldn't see.

"What kind of evidence?"

"The underwear. Text messages."

"Text messages? Who's the woman, do you know her?"

Imani scoffed, "Woman? Try women. I know he's cheated on me with at least three."

"Jeez."

"I know."

"Imani, you need to let him go. Like... Forever."

"I already broke up with him!"

Franco rested his hand on Imani's arm, "No. I'm serious Imani. You've broken up with Brian before but you need to make it permanent this time, okay? Don't get roped back in."

"I won't!"

Franco shot Imani a look of disbelief. She knew she'd earned that bad reputation given her prior history with Brian.

"You seem calm Imani. Too calm. If you really thought it was over with Brian, wouldn't you be tearful? Wouldn't you be making plans to give his stuff back?"

She knew Franco was eyeing the Yale sweatshirt she was wearing. Maybe he had a point.

"I am serious Franco."

"Okay... Maybe we should study then since you have it all under control."

Franco reached for his messenger bag, but Imani jut her hand out to stop him.

"Wait," Imani said, "Tell me why everyone hates Brian..."

Franco chuckled, "Oh, so you think I'm a dummy then? Listen cupcake, I'm not going to compromise my class rank by reading my study buddy for filth about the guy she's dating."

"I don't get it!" Imani huffed, exasperated.

"I'll tell you if you ask me again. But you have to promise me that you have what it takes to handle the truth."

Imani pouted, but her curiosity was pounding in her chest. She had to know. After all the whispers, the judgmental looks and the snide remarks that she'd endured about her relationship, Imani finally wanted to know what people were saying about her and Brian.

"Tell me!"

Franco sighed, "Imani... Brian is racist."

Imani laughed. She laughed and laughed and then looked at Franco after realizing that he wasn't laughing along with her.

"What? You can't be serious Franco."

"I'm serious."

"Hello? Franco? I'm black?"

"Really? Hadn't noticed?"

Imani smacked him playfully and replied, "Franco, I'm serious."

"Girl, I am serious. Your girlfriends stopped hanging out with you because he makes these racial remarks towards them."

"That's not possible."

"Yeah? Well I'm telling you that I know, he called Kim's hair nappy and he asked Claire if he could call her a 'half-negro'."

"What?!"

"Still think I'm lying? Call them. I'm sure Kim will be happy to tell you everything that's wrong with Brian."

"But is that it then?"

Imani had a feeling that Brian's secret life of inappropriate comments was just the tip of the iceberg.

"Oh you know that isn't it..."

"I want to know more... Please... You have to help me Franco..."

"I still don't believe this will stop you from going back to him."

"Why not?!"

"Because I know you Imani. And I know Brian. He knows exactly what he has to do to win you back. And when he wants you, that's what he'll do."

"So you think I'm weak?"

"No. I think you're very strong. I think you're brilliant. I think you'll be Dr. Raymond and graduate in the top of your class. But I know that your dating life has always been messy. It's just the truth, Imani."

Imani sighed. Franco had a point, even if she didn't want to admit it.

"Tell me more about Brian... I need to know everything Franco."

Franco had stories. Loads of stories. As she listened more and more, Imani began to think that she was dealing with a man who led a double life. She almost couldn't believe everything that Franco said about him. This wasn't Brian. It couldn't have been! Sure, he was critical about Imani's weight, her academics and whether she would be a suitable wife, but it was normal for boyfriends to fuss. Right?

By the time Franco was done, Imani looked at him as if she were about to cry. Franco's eyed filled with pity.

"I don't need pity right now Franco," Imani huffed.

"Sorry. Sorry. Didn't mean to pity you it's just that... I get it Imani..."

"Get what?"

"I get why you put up with him. But you don't have to."

"What do you know about what women put up with?"

Franco shifted in his seat uneasily.

"Listen. Just… try not to take him back okay? He isn't good for you and you know it."

"He inspires me! To be a better person."

"He criticizes you," Franco corrected, "And since when has anyone become a better person because of a bully?"

"You know what?" Imani said, "I don't want to talk about this anymore. Talk about something else. Tell me about work."

"Well," Franco started, "There might be a position opening up for an intern in the next few months. If you take it, I guarantee by the time you graduate there will be something bigger."

"Really?" Imani's eyes lit up. She could always trust Franco to bring her the good news as well as the bad.

"Yes, really," He said, "And I know you're near the top of your class Imani. If you get this job, you'll be sailing smoothly after grad school."

Imani enjoyed the fantasy. But then she thought of Brian. Brian had told her that she shouldn't work herself to death while in grad school, or she'd burn out. He'd told her to wait until they'd decided where to move before thinking about work after grad school. Given all that Franco had said about Brian, was it possible that all of that had been a clever hoax to keep Imani stagnant?

After a few more hours of studying and chatting, Imani said goodbye to Franco. As he left, she wondered what it would be like if Franco was her boyfriend. Imani grossed herself out at the thought immediately after it crossed her mind. Franco was a good friend, but he wasn't boyfriend material. They were too close. Imani wondered what kind of girl Franco did date. He'd never mentioned any girls to her or introduced her to any of his girlfriends, if he'd had any.

In the days after Franco left, Imani was readjusting to her life without Brian. She understood why he'd been so militant about warning her not to get back together with Brian. Now that she was beginning to grasp what it was truly like to be alone for the first time in years, Imani was starting to mourn her boyfriend.

Sure, Brian was a little critical but he spent time with her. He listened to her. He talked to her. Plus, Brian was a very liberal spender. He ensured that Imani had the best of everything she wanted. He hadn't called her to ask her to return any of the gifts — as far as Imani was concerned, that was a point in his favor.

After two weeks passed after the break up, Imani began to wonder why Brian hadn't called her. Why wasn't he groveling and trying to win her back? She wondered if he'd really moved on that easily, or if he was doing this on purpose, and stubbornly waiting on Imani to make the first move.

While Imani was at a café with Franco, Brian called her for the first time since their breakup. Franco glanced at her phone and saw the name flash across the screen.

"Do not answer it," Franco hissed, snatching Imani's phone off the table.

"Franco! Give it back!"

Franco held her phone out of reach until it rang out.

"Well, now I have to call him back."

"Do not call him back!"

"It's been two weeks since we broke up Franco and he's calling me for the first time. Shouldn't I hear him out?"

"Can't you see that this is all part of his game Imani? First, he starves you out. Then, you come back groveling."

"I'm not groveling!" Imani insisted.

"Yeah, only because I won't let you."

Imani pouted and stuck her nose back into her book.

"Oh, don't get all pissy."

"I'm not pissy! I'm just... annoyed. You don't know what it's been like these past few weeks."

"Liberating?"

"No," Imani replied with a scowl, "Lonely."

"Loneliness isn't an excuse to get into a relationship Imani."

"Easy for you to say. You're some kind of weird super-human who doesn't even rely on human contact."

"That's not true."

"Yeah?" Imani said, "Then how come I've never seen you with a woman?!"

Franco chuckled, "Imani... Really?"

"What?" Imani looked at him puzzled.

"Imani, I'm gay..."

Imani's eyes widened. She'd never really thought about it before, but it sort of made sense.

"Wait... But how come you don't do... gay... things...."

Franco laughed, "Come on Imani... Just because I don't fit into your tired stereotype of what a gay man should be doesn't mean that I'm not gay..."

Imani realized that Franco was right. She'd made lots of assumptions about him; those assumptions were probably a big part of the reason why he hadn't told her he was gay in the first place.

"Sorry... You're right... I'm stupid..."

"No... Not stupid. Just ignorant. And I do need human interaction. I'm just private about it. Years of hiding who you are will do that to you."

Imani suddenly started perceiving her friend with far more depth than she'd realized. Franco was big, burly, handsome and a genius at environmental science. Still, because of who he chose to sleep with, he was walking on eggshells constantly, worried about what he would lose if he dared to reveal who he truly was.

Still, Imani was preoccupied with the fact that Brian had called. Once she and Franco had finished up at the café, she struggled with the temptation to call Brian back. She knew that Franco would be pissed off if she did. But this wasn't about Franco... It was about her. It was about the life she wanted to have.

Imani couldn't have that life alone. She also didn't want to jump back into the world of dating and start all the way over from scratch while she was trying to finish up her graduate program. Just when she was at her weakest, Brian called again and this time, Imani couldn't resist picking up. If he'd cheated, maybe they could move past it. People moved past cheating all the time. If they were serious, they should be able to handle anything...

"Brian?"

"Hey Imani," He said, "How are you holding up?"

"Fine," Imani said, her voice cracking already.

She couldn't bear how foolish she felt. She couldn't bear the crippling loneliness that had latched onto her since the breakup. Imani had tried to force herself to believe that she didn't need a man. She hated how crumbling and needy she felt whenever it came to Brian.

"You don't sound fine Imani. Why don't I come over."

"Brian, we're broken up," Imani replied weakly.

"I know that. Does it mean that I can't comfort you as a friend?"

Imani let out a long, loud sigh. She could feel herself getting roped back in, even if she reminded herself that Brian was bad for her. Even if she reminded herself that she should have more self-respect than to allow a man who had cheated on her to get back into her life.

"Fine. But there won't be any funny business Brian."

"Of course not. I'll be there in ten."

Imani hung up and guilt clutched at her heart. She knew if Franco were here, he'd be pretty close to smacking her for actually going through with this.

"It's my life," Imani whispered to herself, "And I can be with whoever I want."

Imani knew she was just going out of her way to justify a bad decision. But if Brian was really a bad guy, she'd be able to see it while he was at her place. Within ten minutes, Brian arrived. Imani watched as he walked out of his car, rounded his way to the backseat and pulled out a giant bouquet of blood red roses.

He was dressed in a suit and his black hair was slicked back. Imani could have swooned — if that were a thing women did anymore. Brian looked good. And prepared. If this was the beginning of "I'm sorry", maybe it was only fair for Imani to hear him out and give him a chance to state his case.

Brian knocked and Imani opened her door before she even heard the second knock.

"Brian... hi..."

"I brought you flowers beautiful," Brian said, handing Imani the bouquet.

Her face couldn't help but light up as she grasped the gorgeous, fragrant bouquet. But Brian had called her "beautiful". If he'd really come here as a "friend", he was off to a bad start. Imani determined that she'd keep her cool and stand her ground when it came to Brian.

She cleared her throat.

"Uh... Thanks Brian. I appreciate it. But I'm serious. We're just friends, nothing more."

Brian turned to face her with a smirk plastered across his face. Imani knew that smirk well. It meant that Brian felt like he was in control of the situation and whatever he wanted, he was almost 100% certain he would get it.

"LISTEN, Imani... I know you think it's best if we're just friends, but... don't you think that's short sighted?" Brian spoke slowly, moving closer and closer towards Imani.

His Armani cologne began to filter into her nostrils. All the fond memories she associated with Brian's scent flooded into her mind and Imani could physically feel her will weakening. She took a step back in an attempt to put distance between them.

"Brian... You cheated on me. And you never apologized."

"Apologized?" Brian's face screwed up in confusion, "Of course I'm sorry Imani... I ruined a relationship with the woman I want to spend the rest of my life with, of course I'm sorry..."

"I need more than that Brian!"

"Imani, I have my needs as a man... I succumbed

to the temptation of women who were just jealous of the connection we had..."

"Brian! Come on... You're going to need a better line than that."

"Marry me," Brian asserted.

"What?!" Imani exclaimed.

"I'm serious. I'll prove to you I'm ready to put these mistakes behind us and focus only on you."

Imani wondered why Brian was dangling marriage in her face all of a sudden. He'd always hinted at it, but she'd never taken him seriously. She thought that marriage was a nice idea to Brian rather than an actual goal.

"You aren't serious... What?!"

Brian got down on one knee and produced a tiny black box from his pocket. Imani was still unsure if Brian was serious or if it was all just some game to him. He'd cheated on her, but if that really meant anything, why would he be ready to propose, ready to take that huge step just to win her back?

"I'm serious," Brian said, opening the box, "I want you to marry me Imani Raymond. I want you to be my beautiful wife. I want nothing in the world to tear us apart. I promise you, I will never leave you."

Imani was skeptical, but she didn't want to say no. Everything was telling her this was a bad idea but the emotions provoked by the sight of an engagement ring put her behavior almost out of her control.

"Yes... I'll marry you Brian," Imani replied, sealing her fate.

Years later...

Flyover Country

Nothing about Oklahoma sounded appealing to Imani when she'd first heard about the assignment. She loved travel and she loved the wilderness but Oklahoma was beyond wild. It wasn't the countryside, the coyotes or the bears she worried about — but the people.

Imani was accustomed to forward thinking urbanites. She was accustomed to having access to corner stores and black hairdressers and places she could go and see her people. If the agency sent her out here, she'd have to spend months around people who could probably go months without seeing someone black, or anyone with color to them. It wasn't that Imani had a problem with the white westerners, she just feared that they'd have a problem with her.

Ever since things had ended with Brian, Imani felt like a town in the middle of nowhere would be the perfect place to heal. Imani tried to get some sleep on the plane instead of thinking of Brian, but it was difficult. Four years of love had been torn apart in an instant and now everything they shared together had evaporated, leaving Imani alone to face life's challenges alone.

Imani had tried everything to convince Brian to stay. She'd offered to learn Korean — the language he spoke. She offered to spend a year in Seoul. She lost twenty pounds. But Brian wanted to leave. That's what Imani had trouble understanding. He didn't care about their cultural differences or about all the promises he'd made to Imani. Brian's father had died leaving him about $700,000 and Brian wanted to travel the world and experience what the world had to offer. Imani was sure a part of that meant becoming a bachelor again and experiencing the fine women too.

The ring he'd given her had been just another trinket. Something to keep her with him until something better caught his eye.

Imani tried not to think about it too much. She tried not to let her self-esteem take the natural dip that comes when your lover of so many years decides that uncertainty is more powerful than his feelings for you. Imani looked towards her work partner on the plane. Franco didn't have to worry about problems like this at all. He didn't seem to be worried about anything. He was sleeping — hard — on the trip to Oklahoma and unbothered by everything. Franco was the one who had finally convinced Imani to take the plunge and leave behind all the drama of the East Coat for six months.

Hung up on self-torture, Imani began to look through the pictures on her phone. Brian was still in many of them. He was tall, handsome, strapping and always had that far off look in his eye like he was thinking about being somewhere else. Now, Imani felt foolish for not noticing. Even looking at pictures of herself, she felt like she was looking at a stranger. She was still short, she was still a deep umber color and she still enjoyed wearing shoulder length wigs in various styles and colors. But she didn't look like herself in those pictures. She was a ghost.

It was as if Franco could sense she was making a bad decision. He'd always been gunning for her to stay away from Brian. As Imani got swept up in deep reminiscence about the relationship that had ended, Franco roused from his slumber.

"Imani... What are you doing?"

"Nothing," She said, too hastily, concealing her

phone under the fleece blanket that was draped over her lap.

"Yeah right. You were obsessing again, weren't you?"

"I wasn't!"

"Give me the phone!"

"What phone?"

Franco reached under Imani's fleece blanket and grabbed onto her phone, swiftly unlocking it. Imani didn't even bother ask how he'd figured out her pass code.

"You need to stop this Imani, okay? It's not healthy! Brian is half-way across the world and now it's your turn to travel and just soak it all in. He's an asshole you need to move on."

Imani scoffed, "Well visiting Oklahoma is hardly backpacking in Tibet..."

"And so fucking what? Brian gave up a chance with you to live out a teenage fantasy. In your thirties, you're supposed to settle down. So I'm going to need you to stop feeling like shit and just prepare for the work we're about to do."

"Right."

"Listen, you're smart Imani. Very smart. Don't let this guy play you."

Franco held onto Imani's phone and then tilted his head back like he was going to sleep again. Imani resented how correct Franco was about all this. He had been there for her when everything started going south. He'd been there for her when she could barely keep it together at work and he'd prevented her from getting fired over it.

Imani tapped Franco's shoulder.

"Mm?"

"Can we at least chat about the project before we land?"

Franco raised his head again and nodded. At least keeping him focused on the science would ensure Imani didn't start "obsessing" over Brian again.

"So John got a call from a group of regional activists that fear this town — Homer — might be in some need of environmental advocacy. There's very little enforced regulation out here and people in neighboring towns are starting to get sick from their water. Someone, somewhere is polluting and we're supposed to find out who they are. And where they are. They think some of the ranches out there might be polluted."

"Great..."

"Well we'll also need to find out if any land owners are being affected by someone else's pollution. They may be entitled to federal compensation."

"Right. So where are we staying out there?"

"There's a small motel and we'll each have separate rooms... Shared kitchen. Gina organized the whole thing. So don't worry, if you meet any sexy cowboys, you'll have a place to take 'em."

"Very funny," Imani said, rolling her eyes.

She didn't think that she'd be taking home any cowboys, sexy or otherwise. A town like Oklahoma probably didn't have any attractive men. They'd all be the kind of guys who smelled like cow manure and had no idea what a subway was. Or something.

After thirty more minutes of science-talk with Franco, Imani noticed the plane descending.

"Almost there," Franco said, "It's going to be real different from New York. Ready to receive the shock of your life?"

Imani nodded.

"Any idea how these people are in terms of politics?"

Franco chuckled, "Let's just say conservative. Their science text book is probably the Old Testament."

"Oh boy. What are we getting into..."

"Just relax Imani. It will be fine. Remember, you can't judge them before you get to know them."

Imani chuckled, "Easy for you to say! I can't hide behind black..."

"You're a smart cookie though. You'll figure out

how to keep these people from getting under your skin."

Once the plane landed, they disembarked on the smallest airport that Imani had ever seen. Then they got into their ordered car towards Homer. The drive there was uneventful. They drove past cornfield after cornfield. Imani starred out the window as Franco made conversation with their driver. Their driver seemed tickled by the presence of rich "city folk". Imani didn't think of herself as rich. But compared to the small towns she saw peppering the dry, rural landscape, she understood where their driver could have come up with that idea.

Imani caught Franco's eyes a couple of times in the rearview mirror. She was worried about how he would fare in Oklahoma too. He had a life back east but he wasn't big into dating. Imani wasn't sure why. Franco was attractive enough. He was tall, cared about nature and the environment as well as a religious weight lifting schedule. He had long brown hair and hazel colored eyes that glimmered whenever he talked about any of his scientific passions.

When they pulled up in front of the hotel, Imani understood why their agency had opted to put them up here for a few months. The costs had to be low, especially for such a long stint. As the car pulled up, the driver turned around and said to Imani.

"You know ma'am, I'm just warning ya to be careful 'round here after dark. Don't be fooled by the small town charm."

Imani wasn't sure what to say so she uttered an uncomfortable, "Thank you," in response.

Franco checked in for them and carried both their bags up to the second floor rooms. They separated ways to enter their bedrooms and begin unpacking. The TV in Imani's room didn't work. Perfect. At least then she could be mostly unplugged from the outside world.

They'd outfitted a special suite for Imani and Franco. Their two rooms were completely separate but they shared an adjoining kitchen and bathroom. They'd definitely be wanting to cook out here. Imani couldn't imagine what sort of restaurants they had, but she doubted they made anything close to what she could cook. Or Franco. Franco made Italian cooking better than any restaurant and he loved cooking too.

Imani unpacked everything. She didn't have much with her. Boots for the field, then a pair of regular sneakers. Jeans to wear in the field. T-shirts. Warm clothes. The tiniest bit of makeup. A spare pare of glasses. Her tablet. Her phone. Her computer. Soil testing kits. A spare wig. Once she was done unpacking, Imani noticed how quiet it was. It felt unusual.

Imani knocked on Franco's door.

"Before dark, can we explore?" She asked as he opened it.

Franco chuckled, "Girl, of course. I'm done unpacking but I need to get a coat."

Franco suited up and then the two of them left the hotel room. Imani felt safer walking through the streets with Franco by her side. They'd been friends for years and Imani had always enjoyed seeing a new place with Franco. He had that fun, exuberant attitude that made the unfamiliar intriguing as opposed to stressful.

Oklahoma was warming up already. April meant that some parts of farming season had started and that buds were just breaking up through the earth and turning their faces towards the sun. Franco wanted to take a car into the downtown area, but Imani insisted upon walking.

The walk proved to be worthwhile. Oklahoma was flat, and in some respects boring, but it was teeming with wildlife unlike anything Imani had ever known. This was the real countryside. There was a sense of divine earth energy here that Imani couldn't help but fall in love with. Just breathing in the air, she felt at peace. If she could just close her eyes and experience this land without the people, and without working, Imani was sure she would love it.

She hadn't been camping much — only for work reasons — but she bet that some places out here had excellent camping grounds.

Once they approached the small town, the natural beauty deconstructed and it turned into a typical tiny town. There were pawn shops, general stores and tattoo parlors that all met on one big Main Street. Well, Main Street was bigger than any other street although it was hardly big compared to Fifth Avenue. Here, there were two restaurants, the Post Office and a library that looked about the size of Imani's East Coast apartment.

As they walked through the streets, she held onto Franco's arm. There weren't many people there, but the ones they ran into shot Imani bizarre looks of disgust. Imani thought she might be losing her head. She had to be imagining the intense stare downs and snarled lips.

"I feel like people are staring at me Franco!" She whispered.

Franco shrugged, "Maybe they are. We're not from 'round here and I bet these people aren't too fond of tourists."

Imani doubted very many tourists came here

anyways. She and Franco walked into a few of the small shops. The clothing was definitely Midwestern. There were wide brimmed hats, leather vests, cowboy boots, cowhide, coonskin caps and more. Nothing that Imani would ever buy — not even as a souvenir.

While they were in one of the little shops, Imani got the distinct sense that they were being followed. Franco seemed oblivious to it all, but Imani could tell that the smallish shop owner had his eyes glued to her back.

"Y'all need anything?" He asked.

Imani jumped out of her skin. The man was standing a few inches behind her at most, almost as if he'd snuck up on them on purpose.

"No, we're just looking around," Franco replied, seeing Imani's surprise and stepping in.

"Lookin' 'round. Right. So y'all don't need help?"

"No thanks."

"Well don't be gettin' up to trouble or stealin' nothing. Us folks 'round here are armed."

He looked Imani dead in her eyes as he said the word "armed". She felt a chill run down her spine. Something about the way he was looking at her just felt off. Before Imani or Franco could respond, a man walked through the door of the shop.

"Jethro!" The man called to the shop owner, "Are you hasslin' these out of towners?"

Jethro turned to face the man who had just walked in with a scowl on his face. Imani could tell instantly that they didn't like each other.

"Why don't you mind yer business? I ain't come into yer place of business and tell you how to run things."

"Just leave 'em alone. They ain't from 'round here but they're with the government."

Jethro didn't seem any more impressed by the revelation that Imani and Franco were with the government. Based on how run-down the town look, Imani could guess that they weren't too thrilled with how things were being run. Government employees wouldn't easily win them over.

"How did you know we were with the government?" Franco asked.

"Easy," The strapping man who had just entered said, "Ain't any tourists in Homer and y'all look like you're here for a reason. Ain't too hard to put two and two together."

The man tipped his hat to Imani and said, "Plus, I know ain't any tourists pretty as this one."

Imani blushed and looked down. The man didn't take his gaze off of her and she felt herself blushing uncontrollably. She hadn't felt so giddy around a man in a long time. Everything about it was unfamiliar. This particular local was handsome too. He had brilliant blue eyes and blonde hair that looked bleached from hours in the sun.

Without giving a name, he continued, "Don't let Jethro here scare you off. He's just afraid of people who don't look like they're from Oklahoma... It's why he married his cousin you see."

"You little son of a bitch..." Jethro muttered, turning bright red.

"M'lady. Hope I run into you again," The man said with a grin, flashing a boyish wink at Imani before leaving the store.

Franco turned towards Jethro who was sputtering madly at the door and said, "Uh... Thanks sir for your time. We'll be heading out."

He grabbed Imani's arm and they left the store. Imani turned back once they were on the street, trying to catch sight of the blond cowboy who had flirted with her in the store.

"Who was that guy?" Imani asked.

"See? I told you that you'd find a nice cowboy," Franco said with a grin.

"Oh shut it. He was just being friendly."

"Uh huh."

"I'm not looking for anything out here Franco. I

just want to test the soil, wait for the results and do our job out here."

Franco smiled. He knew that getting Imani to actually cut loose would be a project and a half. She was determined to be stoic and reserved. Franco knew that she'd been burned pretty badly by Brian, but he still wanted her to at least get a start on moving on. Hell, Brian had certainly moved on. Franco hadn't bothered to tell Imani how much he knew about that.

"Nothing wrong with having a little fun," Franco replied.

They took the long way back to the hotel. Imani listened patiently as Franco talked about how excited he was to take a look at some of the flora and fauna of Oklahoma. Well, Imani tried to listen. Really, she was thinking about what had happened between her and Jethro, the store owner.

Once she was safely in her room, Imani decided to do a little more homework on Homer, Oklahoma. When she'd jumped into the assignment, she hadn't actually researched much about the town. She knew Franco wouldn't take no for an answer and she wanted to just do something spontaneously for once in her life. But Imani had to admit this was more than just her prejudices about small town folks. Something about the people in this town gave her the creeps. The way Jethro had practically threatened her felt off too. In fact, as far as Imani could tell, the only normal person in the town was the guy who had come to their rescue in Jethro's store.

Imani typed "Homer Oklahoma" into her search engine and the first result sent chills down her spine.

"10 Sundown Towns Black Travelers Should Veer Away From".

Imani clicked on the link and saw Homer sitting at #4 on the list. Sundown towns. Oh boy. Imani flopped back in bed and wondered what she had gotten herself into. Tomorrow she'd have to head to work at the various ranches around town and she'd have to face the people in this town without showing just how terrified she was.

About twenty minutes later, Franco knocked on Imani's door.

"Yes?"

"Can I come in?"

"Sure," Imani replied, letting out a long sigh.

She allowed Franco to enter her bedroom and sat up on bed. Imani shut the laptop. Franco had such a positive attitude about the town and she didn't want to ruin it by worrying him. Franco joined her, sitting at the foot of her bed. He was looking at her with a stern, fatherly expression.

Franco said nothing for a while and Imani was forced to break the silence.

"Yes?"

"I came here to check on you. I know you're taking the break up with Brian hard and... I wanted to see if you needed to talk."

Imani sighed. Of course she needed to talk.

"Remember that night Brian cheated on me?"

Franco chuckled.

"Yes. How could I forget?"

"After that night, I convinced myself that I wouldn't take Brian back. I convinced myself that cheating was the last straw. But still. I accepted more. I just kept taking and taking... I kept destroying parts of myself for him and now I just feel empty."

"Brian was an asshole."

"I know but... You don't understand Franco. You don't understand how hard it is for me to get over him. You don't get the magnetism..."

Franco nodded.

"Wanna go outside? I need a smoke."

"Sure."

Imani wrapped the fleece blanket around her shoulders, slipped into her bedroom slippers and followed Franco onto the motel balcony. The "vacancies" sign was glowing bright red (except it was missing the letters c,n, and i). Imani wouldn't have been surprised if they were the only guests at the hotel. She doubted that Homer received many visitors.

Franco slipped into his pocket and pulled out a packet of Marlboros. He lit up and offered some to Imani which she politely declined.

"You know," Franco said after taking a long drag, "I understand you and Brian better than you think. I get you Imani. I get what you love about Brian. First of all, he wasn't hard on the eyes. He was smart too. And he always made you feel like if you were with him, somehow you were better than other people. Isn't that right?"

Imani nodded. She hadn't expected him to, but Franco understood her attraction to Brian better than most people.

"He wasn't afraid of anything and because of that, you felt like you were untouchable too, right?"

She nodded again.

"But none of that was real Imani. I'm just telling you this as a friend... Not to be an asshole. None of it was real. Brian played you because that's what he does and it's not your fault."

"It's not my fault," Imani whispered. She wasn't sure if she was convinced. But she appreciated Franco's commitment to trying.

She wrapped her arms around Franco and gave him a big hug. He continued to smoke with one hand and hugged Imani with his other arm.

"So what? Oklahoma is supposed to be a fresh start?"

Franco laughed.

"Yes. Why don't you try going after that tasty cowboy."

"Franco! No!"

Franco laughed again.

"We'll see I guess... I bet there are quite a few other sexy farmhands in this part of town..."

Franco finished his cigarette, had another one, and then they both turned in for the night. Even if Homer sent a shiver traveling down Imani's spine, she was starting to have some kind of hope that this could be her fresh start. At least here, there was no way she could get lured in by Brian's silver tongue again. She would show him that she could thrive without him. She didn't need to keep destroying her life to uplift Brian's.

Imani slept better than she ever had on the east coast. While Imani found the sounds of the city comforting, there was something peaceful about the silence of the countryside. Instead of blaring sirens and screaming citizens, there were crickets and roosters.

The next morning, Imani knew she'd have a hard day ahead. She welcomed the challenge. At least during the day time here, she didn't have to worry as much. Imani didn't want to think about what happened (or what could happen) in the town after dark. The sun was brighter here and the sky was totally cloudless. Imani could smell Franco cooking breakfast in their shared kitchen. He must have gone out early to pick up supplies. Looking at her watch, Imani saw that she only had ninety minutes until work. Crap.

She hopped in the shower and then dressed, adding a shoulder length wig to complete her field-work outfit. Imani opted for her glasses rather than her contacts and then she opened the door to the kitchen where Franco was preparing breakfast.

"Hey gorgeous!" Franco boomed.

"Hey," Imani mumbled.

She didn't exactly have Franco's enthusiasm for mornings. But he'd finished making breakfast and he'd made a giant pot of coffee, so Imani figured she could forgive him. She allowed Franco to serve out breakfast and they ate together while Franco discussed their agenda for the day. Imani had barely checked her email so she appreciated Franco's update.

Their first order of business for the day was to

visit ranches and ask the ranch owners to allow them to test the soil. Their rental car had been delivered to the motel overnight, so they wouldn't be restricted to walking for the duration of their trip. After breakfast, they packed up their field equipment and drove the hybrid Toyota Prius towards the first ranch they'd been directed to.

"Do you think these people are really going to allow us onto their land?"

"Dunno," Franco said.

"Well, we stick out like a sore thumb. I'm black and you're —," Imani started.

"I know, I know," Franco interrupted before she could finish, "Though I think we should just try to... blend in."

Imani realized that Franco was just as nervous as she was. Knowing that at least she was not alone made Imani feel a bit better. They'd have to work on blending into Homer's small-town social scene together.

They arrived at the first ranch they were supposed to be visiting. The acres of the ranch stretched about as far as Imani's eye could see. The vast expanses of open terrain in Oklahoma amazed Imani. She considered herself more of a city girl — and definitely an east coast girl — but there was something awe-inspiring about the open land, the fresh air and the blue skies.

They parked and Franco led the way to the house sitting in the middle of a big field.

"Think anyone will answer the door?" Imani asked.

"They might just shoot us for trespassing."

Imani froze.

"Geez, I'm just kidding Imani."

"Very funny," She replied sarcastically.

Franco approached the large doors of the ranch and knocked a few times. There was no response. Imani was beginning to get nervous. What if Franco's little joke came true. She already knew that this town had a dark, seedy underbelly. If there were any black folk around here, they probably lived in fear.

Imani had found it a little troubling that she hadn't seen a single person with her skin color or anywhere close.

"I'll call the number I was given," Franco said, fumbling for his phone.

Imani looked around the ranch while Franco called and saw a rumbling tractor approaching in the distance. The line rang out and by the time Franco rang the number again, the tractor was close to them. Now, Imani could see the man who was riding in the tractor — it was the same nameless gentleman who had stopped the store owner Jethro from getting rude with her and Franco.

"Howdy!" He called, stopping his tractor and leaping out of it.

Franco turned around swiftly and shut his phone, slipping it into his pocket. The man walked up to Imani and stuck out his hand. Imani reached her hand out and felt the firmest handshake she'd ever experienced.

"Ajax. Ajax Redford."

"Imani. Imani Raymond."

"Pleasure to meet you," Ajax replied, finally letting go of Imani's hand.

There was electricity where their palms touched. Imani swore she was imagining things. When Ajax looked into her eyes, she detected something else besides interest in meeting her. His eyes seemed hungry for her from the very moment they'd made eye contact.

Ajax kept staring at her even as he shook Franco's hand and introduced himself. Ajax. Imani liked the name. And Franco had been right — he was easy on the eyes too. Ajax was tall, with electric blue eyes and a wide smile. His hair was bleached from the sun and his skin was tanned from hours of tending the ranch. He was dressed for work in the field with khakis and a red plaid shirt that stood out against his tanned skin.

"I'm the ranch manager here. My paw owns this ranch and three others in Oklahoma. One in Idaho."

"Right... So you're his son and the manager here?"

"Yup. Pay's pretty good plus there ain't much sense working for anyone else out here."

"Makes sense," Franco said.

"So... What are y'all city slickers doing 'round here?"

Imani wanted to chuckle at Ajax's use of the phrase "city slickers" but she held back. She found his Western country ways to have a particular charm around them.

"We're with a government environmental advocacy agency and we're wondering if you'd allow us to test some of your soil for toxins, pollutants and heavy metals."

"Government? Mind if I see some ID?"

"Sure," Franco and Imani said in unison, both procuring their federally issued identification.

Ajax seemed to scrutinize their IDs for a bit then he nodded as if he was satisfied by the evidence they'd brought forth.

"Looks good. So where do y'all need to test? I can show y'all 'round the ranch a bit first if that helps."

"That would be great. Thank you sir," Franco said.

"Please... Ajax is fine. I ain't no 'sir'," Ajax replied.

Franco shrugged and the two of them began to follow Ajax as he gave them a tour of the ranch. The ranch was beautifully kept. There were a few hands working diligently as Ajax gave them a tour. There were horses, a few chickens and a few cows and pigs. There was a little guesthouse that Ajax apparently rented out to guests a quarter mile away from the main house.

Imani was taking in the breathtaking landscape and wondering what it would be like to live like this. Ajax had work to do, sure, but he spent most of his time riding on tractors or horses, breathing in the fresh Midwestern air. Plus, it was clear his family owned plenty of land. Rich, arable land.

Once they were back at the main house, Ajax turned to Franco and said, "Why don't y'all test different parts of the ranch? You can head over to the fields behind the guest house and take Roscoe with you. I'll head over towards the horses with Imani."

Franco smirked, "Sure."

Roscoe was one of the younger ranch hands; he couldn't have been older than eighteen. He began to lead Franco away and Imani was left alone with

Ajax. He couldn't have been more blatant about orchestrating time to spend with her alone.

When Ajax saw Imani, he saw a woman unlike any that he'd known in Oklahoma. Her heavy East Coast accent was sweet and lilting. Her physique was beautiful and she just looked amazing in her cute glasses, with her face all scrunched up as she eyed the ranch. Ajax could tell how out of place she was here, but she approached that unfamiliarity with an air of curiosity.

Once Franco was out of earshot, Ajax led Imani to the corner of the ranch she was supposed to test.

"So. How are you liking Homer?"

"It's different. It's quiet," Imani said, crouching down so she could start to prepare her soil samples.

Ajax crouched down next to her, "Different? How so?"

"It's quiet. Just quiet, everywhere. And there are no bodegas, no beauty supply stores, no universities."

"We got a university near by! It's a five hour drive east!"

Imani chuckled, "See? You think a five hour drive is nearby."

She began to scoop her samples into her tubes.

"Is everyone out East as beautiful as you are?"

Imani chuckled. She saw right through Ajax's

55

pick up line. She was flattered, but on her knees collecting soil samples wasn't exactly where she planned to meet her next date.

"Back East, everyone looks like a super model. I'm just a regular girl."

"Well if I'd known that, maybe I would've moved to New York," Ajax replied with a wink.

She twisted the test tube cover on tightly and slipped it back into her sample bag.

"I'm all done here. Could we head to another part of the ranch?"

"Sure thing. You got a boyfriend back East?" Ajax asked as they started walking in another direction.

Jeez. This guy was bold. And relentless. Imani had to admit that she enjoyed being pursued, even if she wasn't too fond of the timing.

"Nope. No boyfriend," Imani replied.

An unexpected pang of sadness hit her chest as she thought about Brian and the heartbreak that had accompanied her breakup.

"What about that guy you came with?"

Imani laughed.

"Franco? Franco is just my coworker. We're good friends. We've been that way for a long time."

"Hm."

"Trust me, there's nothing going on there," Imani replied with a smile.

"So, you're available then?"

Imani crouched down in her new patch of soil and began to fill her vials. She didn't know where to begin to answer that question. Technically, she was available but emotionally, Imani knew she was a mess.

"I guess. Sort of…"

"Listen, I know I'm being real forward with you but it's just… You don't see many beautiful women like you come into town. Just… Wow. Take it as a compliment."

Imani smiled. She did take it as a compliment. Ajax was gorgeous and she could tell he was strong too. As they walked around the ranch together, she noticed his muscles bulging through his shirt. He was different from men in New York in the best way too. He wasn't overly cerebral. He worked with his hands and spent all day in the sun. He knew his way around tractors, he knew his way around the earth. He had a sense of wisdom about his raw masculinity that Imani found very appealing.

If there was any guy who could help her get over Brian, it would be a guy like Ajax. He had that wild and untamed aura that could really allow her some release from her tense, messy life. Still, Imani was wary about letting any guy get too close. Her romantic life had been filled with one romantic mistake after another. At some point, she'd just have to say 'enough is enough'.

"Thanks. I appreciate it."

She collected her soil samples and then stood up to face Ajax. He was looking at her with pure lust in his eyes. Panicked, Imani found her eyes darting around, making sure no one's eyes were on them. She was free to do whatever she liked out here, but that didn't mean she wanted to make a fool out of herself while she was supposed to be engaged in government business.

Ajax took a step closer to Imani and she froze. Her deep cocoa colored eyes locked with Ajax's blue eyes and she felt heat rising to her face. Ajax kissed her cheek and then pulled away.

"So pretty scientist. Wanna tell me where you're staying?"

Imani sputtered and mumbled. At this point, she had to admit to herself that she wanted Ajax. She still couldn't figure out how this had happened. She barely knew a thing about him, yet she didn't stop him from kissing her on the cheek. In fact, his kiss on the cheek felt right.

It still felt inappropriate to tell him where she stayed. What if he came over? What if he asked her out? Then what? Feeling attraction was one thing, but acting on it was another thing entirely. She'd already gone too far with a man she barely knew. She was already feeling an attraction to Ajax that didn't align with how well she knew him.

"I..."

"It's probably the old motel near the highway, huh?"

Imani bit her lower lip. There really were no secrets in a town like this.

"Listen, I won't tell your buddy over there. I just want to see you again once you're done getting your hands dirty."

Imani nodded.

"Sure... Yeah..."

She didn't know what else to do and she didn't have the desire or the willpower to steer Ajax away. He was in hot pursuit of her and Imani had the strong feeling that she would succumb to him.

Country Boys

After they'd received permission from fifteen ranches, Franco and Imani sent the soil samples via express mail at the local post office. As the sun creeped down over the horizon, Imani felt the hairs on the back of her neck standing up. She still hadn't told Franco about what happened after dusk in Homer.

"Let's get out of here," She mumbled as they left.

Franco drove back to the motel quickly and they had a quiet dinner together. Imani knew Franco well enough to know he was tired from traipsing around the ranches all day.

"So, are you meeting up with that cowboy tonight?" Franco asked with an impish smirk on his face.

"No! Why would you say that?"

"Oh come on. He tried to get that alone time with you today and I know you're into him. I can just tell."

"I'm not 'into' him. I just met him."

"So? That's not how attraction works Imani. You can't control it."

"Well. I can control it."

Franco scoffed, "Need I remind you how many times you got back together with Brian?"

"Please," Imani sighed, "Can we do anything except talk about Brian? He's the last person I want to think about."

"Sorry."

"No. It's fine..."

"Listen, the best way to get over someone, is to get involved with someone else..."

"Shouldn't you be experienced enough to know that rebounding is always a bad idea?"

Franco shrugged.

"Is it a bad idea if you have a once in a lifetime chance to have no strings attached with a cowboy? You know country guys have no inhibitions. He can probably do things to you that no New York guy can..."

"Stop!" Imani said, laughing.

Franco could be over-the-top sometimes.

"Well...Maybe if I see him again, I'll give him a chance."

"Psht... I know you will. Come on Imani. There are probably three eligible bachelors in this town."

Imani hated to admit that Franco was probably right about this one. But that didn't mean she'd have to throw herself at the first available man in sight. Imani had learned from her past experiences that her instincts with men were not to be trusted. She could be overly naïve, trusting to a fault, and willing to overlook flaws because of her romantic notions.

"What do you think Brian is doing right now?" Imani mused.

Franco wrinkled his nose, "Brian? I thought you didn't want to talk about Brian."

"I know," Imani said wistfully, "I guess I'm just wondering if he misses me. If he thinks about me. If he's safe."

"Listen. You need to stop thinking about him Imani. It's time for Brian to be gone. You have to start living for you... See? You really do need a rebound."

IMANI THOUGHT about what Franco said, even as she let him change the subject. He began to chatter excitedly about the running trails roping around Homer that he hoped to check out in the afternoon, as well as the ecological analysis they were going to get into the next day. After a long, long chat, Franco retired to bed. Imani knew he was probably just going to read science journals alone, but she appreciated the alone time herself.

As Imani settled into bed with a book, she heard a soft knock at her door. Imani felt chills running down her spine.

"Franco?"

"Nope. It's me, Ajax."

Imani relaxed instantly, realizing that her response represented extreme anxiety about being black in Homer, Oklahoma.

"Oh... Ajax... Is everything alright?"

"Mind if I come in ma'am?"

Imani walked to the door and looked out the peephole. It really was him. She unlocked her door and then cracked it. Ajax stood there beaming. He cleaned up nicely from when she'd seen him earlier at the ranch. He was no longer covered in sweat, though his tan had deepened since the morning.

. . .

His blond hair was wet and slicked back like he'd just hopped out of the shower. Ajax wore a blue, flannel shirt tucked into his dark brown Carhartt pants. Imani could tell that he'd tried to clean his boots — still leaving a little dirt around the bottoms. Seeing his well-dressed appearance and smelling his cologne, Imani decided to let Ajax in.

The worst that could happen was they'd talk for a while and if she wasn't interested in him, she'd tell him that she had to retire for the night.

"Didn't take you too long to find me, did it?"

"Nope. Only one motel 'round here. Y'all must have got the presidential suite or something."

"Really?" Imani chuckled.

The room was nice enough but it hardly counted as "presidential".

"I came over 'cause I got something important to tell you about that government work you're doing."

Imani's curiosity was piqued. She hadn't assumed Ajax's visit had anything to do with work or business.

"What do you have to tell me?"

"Got any water 'round here? A fella could use a drink."

Imani had been so busy staring at Ajax and analyzing him upon entry that she'd forgotten every modicum of politeness. Now, she felt embarrassed that she hadn't offered Ajax a seat or a drink.

"Yeah... Uh... sure... Where are my manners. Why don't you have a seat."

Imani hastened towards the sink in the shared kitchen and poured herself and Ajax a tall glass of water. From what she could hear, Franco was fast asleep. Or being very quiet.

Imani handed Ajax the glass of water and then sat across from him.

"So... What is it you have to tell me."

"Y'all are here testing for environmental pollution right?"

"Yeah. Something like that. We work to protect at risk areas where the populations don't have advocacy of their own."

Ajax snickered, "Well, Homer's always been a lawless land."

Imani listened intently, wondering what on earth Ajax meant by lawless.

He continued, "There's something going on here Imani... I know it... All the other ranchers are gonna pretend like it's all okay but let's just say not everyone plays by the rules."

"And what about you? You play by the rules?" Imani asked, removing her glasses and setting them to the side.

Ajax laughed, "I play by the rules when I can see the benefit in it."

Imani didn't understand what Ajax meant by that. But she could tell from the way he was looking at her that they were no longer talking about the details of environmental destruction and ranch life.

She changed the subject.

"So what do you know about how your ranch complies with the federal regulations?"

Ajax laughed, "Is it this hard for you to unwind all the time?"

Imani scrunched up her face. What exactly did Ajax want from her? As hard as he was trying to flirt, she was in Oklahoma on business. She didn't exactly appreciate his insinuations about her personality when he really didn't know a thing about her!

"How would you know what I'm like all the time?" Imani snapped.

Ajax looked down, "Didn't mean to offend you ma'am. I just... Well... I'm trying to get to know you."

He was still looking at her with that lustful look. Imani remembered what Franco had advised her to do while she was out here, and she softened her demeanor just a little bit.

"Well... What do you want to know about me," Imani replied with a smile.

Ajax looked back at her surprised, as if he hadn't

expected her demeanor to soften that quickly. Imani knew she could try to be more relaxed around Ajax. Truth be told, there was nothing about him that made her uncomfortable. It was her attraction to him that sat uneasy in her chest. Ajax was different from every man she'd ever known. He came from a small, definitely racist town in Oklahoma. Could she really put aside their differences and just allow her feelings to carry her forward? Was that a strategy that could really work out in her favor.

"I want to know why you decided to come to Homer?"

Imani shrugged.

"I don't know, Franco convinced me that it would be good for me. I just got through a bad breakup so I guess I needed the change of pace."

"Franco... Are you and him..."

Imani laughed.

"Me and Franco? No. I already told you! Let's just say, he's not interested in me. I'm sure of it."

"Hm," Ajax seemed disbelieving.

Ajax continued, "But about this breakup..."

Imani shook her head, "Oh no. I don't want to talk about it... I promised myself I wouldn't bring that drama out here."

"So you won't tell me what kind of idiot dumps a girl like you?"

Imani chuckled, "A girl like me? What do you know about me?"

"I know you're beautiful. And you must be smart. And you seem like a real classy lady."

"Well, thank you," Imani looked down shyly.

"Listen, if you ever run into problems 'round town, you come find me. I'll help you out."

"Thanks," Imani said.

She stood up and then grabbed their empty glasses, taking them to the sink. While she was at the sink, she heard Ajax get up and figured he was headed for the door. When she turned around and came face to face with him, Imani realized that she was wrong.

"Ajax," She started.

"Sh," He interrupted her, "Don't say a word."

Ajax planted his lips on hers and then pulled away. Imani stared at him wide-eyed. A kiss? So soon? Her attraction to Ajax was there, but Imani had been trying her best to conceal any signs that she had feelings for him.

"I told you, I don't play by the rules," Ajax said.

His accent sounded so hot. Imani tried to resist looking into his hypnotic blue eyes, but she found herself drawn to his gaze. Ajax leaned forward and kissed her again. This time, she wrapped her arms around Ajax and kissed him deeply. This time, when Imani pulled away, she looked frightened.

"Sh... Don't be scared..." Ajax whispered.

She closed her eyes and kissed him again before pulling away.

"I can't do this Ajax... I... I... I'm supposed to be here for work," She whispered.

"And what? You're not allowed to have a little fun."

"I'm not like you... I always play by the rules," Imani urged.

Ajax grinned, "Well I don't. And I also go after what I want... relentlessly... I know you want me too Imani. Just let it happen..."

Every sensible notion in Imani's brain was telling her to resist Ajax. But staring him in the eyes, she knew she was going to pursue a different path. Maybe Ajax had a point. Maybe playing by the rules had too often led to major problems in her life. Imani just wanted to feel good. She just wanted to feel wanted. And with Ajax, she felt wanted for the first time in a long time.

"Screw it," Imani whispered, wrapping her arms around Ajax and kissing him again.

As she kissed him, his hands began to rove all over her body. He felt up her chest, her hips, her waist, and eventually, his palms gripped Imani's buttocks tightly. He massaged her flesh repeatedly until Imani let out an unwilling moan.

With an impish grin fully spread across his face, Ajax lifted Imani up onto the counter. Now, they were face to face. Ajax still held her tightly, still kept his lips pressed to hers, while her hands roamed over his chest. She could feel Ajax's rock hard abs through his shirt and she could feel his bulge throbbing at the point where their hips met.

His bulge pressed into her, hot, hard and eager for more. Imani took off her shirt and Ajax then bent his head to her nipples. He grazed his tongue over her bra and she could feel the moist heat from his mouth teasing and tantalizing her nipples. His bulge continued to throb in his pants as he reached behind Imani's back and unhooked her bra.

Imani briefly wanted to stop herself from continuing to kiss Ajax. She knew nothing about him except for the fact that he was a very sexy rancher with a caring tone of voice and a suave demeanor. He could be anyone... He could do anything to her... including hurt her.

"Kiss me," Imani whispered breathily.

Ajax took one of her nipples into his mouth and swirled his tongue repeatedly around her breast. Imani sighed and bit down on her lower lip as Ajax moved his head to her other breast. When he was done lavishing her nipples with kisses, Ajax moved his head back up to Imani's neck.

He grabbed a piece of her flesh between his lips and sucked on it hard. Imani felt wetness pooling between her thighs and she realized that she was heading straight towards sleeping with Ajax. She didn't even want to stop herself at this point. It just felt good to be kissed, to be touched, to have a long, slow buildup to lovemaking. Usually, sex with Brian wasn't half as romantic.

Ajax slipped off his shirt and Imani saw his tanned flesh up close for the first time. She ran her hands down his chest and Ajax chuckled.

"Like what you see?"

Imani nodded, hypnotized by Ajax's 8-pack muscles, broad chest and even more impressive shoulders. Nothing about his strength was a hoax. Ajax started to remove his pants and boxers, sliding them to the ground. Imani gasped as she saw his hardness spring into view. Ajax's dick was big. Not just bigger than average, but much bigger than average.

"Is this how they make 'em in Oklahoma?" She gasped.

Ajax chuckled, "What are you talking about missy?"

"Nothing," Imani muttered, pressing her lips to his again.

As she sat on the counter, she found herself eagerly anticipating a good pounding. She didn't care that Franco was right next door. She didn't care that she was sitting on her kitchen counter. She urgently needed Ajax's thick, powerful member between her thighs.

Franco began to ease Imani out of her pants too and then he slipped her underwear to the side to catch a full glimpse of her wetness. Imani's pussy was bare, except for a small strip of hair. She was sopping wet with anticipation. Before slipping his hardness between her pussy lips, Franco took an index finger and slid it easily into Imani's tightness.

Imani gasped loudly as Franco began to thrust his finger in and out of her wetness. Her tight pussy gripped his finger and Franco began to dexterously pleasure her, finding the most sensitive walls of her pussy and touching them gently with his fingers. Imani clung to Franco as he began to pleasure her furiously.

She bucked her hips to meet his fingers and moaned. She could feel Franco's desires mounting as he began to plunge his fingers in and out of her wetness at an even faster rate.

"Yes..." She whimpered.

"Want more?"

Did she?

Imani couldn't believe how swiftly she'd gotten swept up in this Oklahoma white boy's world. She nodded and began to paw at Ajax's crotch. She urged his hardness to move swiftly between her thighs and deliver all the pleasure she believed him capable of delivering.

"Please..." Imani moaned, "Give it to me Ajax."

She didn't know what came over her. Ajax had unlocked this "naughty" side to her that she never even knew existed. Usually, Imani was tame, polite and always classy. In the short time she'd known Ajax, she already felt free to express her wild, untamed sexuality free from judgment.

Ajax fumbled for a condom and began to sheath his exposed cock. Imani was practically drooling as she watched Ajax struggle to fit his thick member into the condom. There was something so sensual about watching him slowly perform that extra step that made their sexual encounter 100% worry free.

Ajax looked towards the door that separated them from Franco.

"Your friend? Ain't you worried he'll hear you?"

Imani looked down shyly, "We should probably move this to the bed then?"

Ajax smirked, "No. We do it right here... Right now..."

She considered protesting, but realized that she really didn't want to. And it wasn't in her best interests anyways.

"Come here," Imani said urgently, grabbing onto Ajax's wrist to prevent him from moving away from her.

"Ah... I thought so..."

Imani moved towards the edge of the counter and spread her legs wide so that he could position his frame between them. Imani felt the hot tip of Ajax's dick pressing into her tightness. Imani clutched his back and then gasped as Ajax began to plunge his full length inside her.

Imani closed her eyes and allowed her mind to focus solely on the pleasure she was receiving. Ajax's dick stretched her entrance as he planted himself fully between her legs. She cried out and dug her nails into his back as his full length was embedded fully between her thighs.

Ajax gripped Imani's butt as she remained full embedded on his dick. Then he began to thrust into her hard and fast. Imani had never had such wild, untamed sex. Her ex had only "done it" with her under specific conditions. She had never let her desires take full control of her. She'd never allowed herself to relax fully and just enjoy sex. She'd never had love making that wasn't sterile. This felt incredible.

"Yes... Yes..." She heaved as Ajax began to plunge into her harder and faster.

Imani could feel Ajax breaking a sweat in the spot where her hands came into contact with his back. She could hear Ajax's labored breathing and feel his thick, hard cock stretching out her pussy with each forceful thrust. He was taking her, dominating her, and enjoying every minute of it. Imani felt loose and liberated sexually in a way she hadn't before.

She gripped Ajax's blond hair and ran her hands down his abs as he pounded away at her wetness. She could feel an orgasm building between her thighs and Imani felt ready to experience the full extent of euphoria that she could.

"Harder..." She urged Ajax with a whisper.

He gripped her ass cheeks tighter and began to bounce Imani up and down on his dick. Imani couldn't hold back and her soft whimpers became loud moans. Franco could have woken up, but Imani was too enveloped in pleasure to notice or care. All she cared about was the immense feeling of pleasure that occupied the area between her thighs.

How could an Oklahoma cowboy who seemed

so soft-spoken and demure handle her like this in the bedroom?

Imani cried out as a climax finally surged through her body. Her thighs wrapped around Ajax's body more tightly and Imani let out a loud moan as she could feel her juices flowing from her wetness. Her pussy clenched tightly around Ajax's dick as she experienced the most mind-blowing orgasm of all time. Imani had never believed it possible to experience climax from penetration alone, but for the first time in her life, she'd known real pleasure.

Ajax continued to plunge into her slowly and purposefully. Imani groaned as with each thrust, her sensitive pussy was exposed to even more pleasure, almost more than she could handle...

Imani came again and Ajax pulled out of her.

"Get on the bed," He demanded.

Imani realized that Ajax was unlocking more secret desires in her than she could even keep track of. She got into bed and lay on her back. Ajax slowly positioned himself between Imani's thighs and began to kiss her. The gentle kisses caused Imani to relax and sink into the bed. Then, Ajax began to kiss Imani's neck. His tender kisses caused her skin to prickle, and her brown skin to grow even more sensitive.

Then, Ajax moved his head to Imani's stomach. At first, she recoiled from Ajax's lips as they pressed against an area of her body she usually felt self-conscious about. Ajax kissed her so tenderly, that eventually, Imani began to relax. Ajax's lips moved down to the area between her thighs.

He kissed her pubic mound and Imani found herself breathing more heavily in anticipation of Ajax's tongue. Imani gasped as Ajax spread her pussy lips apart and began to plant his tongue on her clit. Her hardened nub engorged from his first touch.

Imani wanted more...

She'd never have a man take a break from his own race to the finish and pleasure her like this. Every touch of Ajax's tongue sent her wild. He began to brush his tongue along the length of her slit with slow, long strokes. Imani groaned in pleasure as Ajax pushed his tongue deeper between her folds. Ajax then began to stroke along her length with furious speed.

Imani gasped and grabbed onto his head, bucking her hips upwards to meet his tongue.

"Yes..." She groaned.

Ajax pressed her hips down hard into the bed and allowed his tongue to stroke her length furiously. Imani climaxed hard. She gasped and grasped at the sheets as her body exploded with ecstasy. Every inch of her skin was on fire with desire for even more of Ajax. She found herself thirsting for his dick in a way she'd never thirsted for another man. If this wasn't just a one time thing, Imani could see her stay in Oklahoma being better than she could have ever imagined...

Ajax brought Imani to another climax and then positioned his dick between her legs again.

"Ohh..." Imani gasped as Ajax began to insert his dick into her wetness again.

She wrapped her legs around Ajax's body, urging him to plunge even deeper into her. Ajax's full length stretched Imani's wetness out again. The heat of Ajax's body pressing into her increased her hunger for an intense pounding.

Ajax began to thrust into Imani harder and faster than before. If he hadn't been determined to finish before, he sure was now. Imani moaned as Ajax's thick cock touched every inch of her pussy. She gyrated and swiveled her hips as Ajax took her hard and fast.

"You like this dick huh?"

"Yes... yes..." Imani moaned breathily.

Ajax took Imani's hands and pinned them down above her head. She wriggled, attempting to pull her way free but Ajax's grip on her was too strong. All

Imani could do was lie still and succumb to his pounding. Ajax began to thrust into her slow and deep. The deeper his strokes, the deeper Imani's pleasure. She felt another release building up inside her. Her yearning for climax propelled her closer and closer towards another orgasm.

"Harder..." She urged again.

Imani could feel Ajax's dick stiffen inside her and she could tell that he was getting close to a climax of his own. She was impressed by how virile Ajax was, how his strength had translated so perfectly in the bedroom. Ajax began to ram his dick into Imani harder, just as she'd asked him to.

Imani climaxed again and she could tell that Ajax was about to finish too. His face scrunched up tightly and he began to grunt as he plunged into Imani's wetness slowly and forcefully. Finally, he emitted a primal groan and Imani could feel his cock twitch two or three more times as he finished. His raw masculine energy encompassed the entire room as he pulled his hardness out of her and then disposed of his sword's latex sheath.

Imani lay on her back, shaken from the experience. She hadn't known that sex could be that good. She hadn't known that sex could take her from stressed out to totally relaxed. Sex had never changed Imani's mindset before. She'd never been allowed the freedom to see it as more than a begrudging duty.

When Ajax returned to bed, he lay beside Imani and she turned to look at him. He was quiet — more quiet than Imani was accustomed to. Then again, it wasn't like Brian was exactly the "gold-standard" for men (or so Imani had learned the hard way.)

In the moment, Imani had felt incredible. But now that she'd come down from her orgasmic high, she was beginning to see her decision to sleep with Ajax in a more judgmental light. He was hot, really hot. But that didn't mean she should try to do this more than once. Ajax was still a man from small town Oklahoma. And Homer was a sundown town, one of the spookier things for Imani to consider.

HE WASN'T USED to seeing black people. Hell, as far as she knew, he held some unsavory political beliefs and her and people like her. If she tried to find out more about Ajax, how could she be anything other than disappointed?

Imani had tried to make it work with one guy who had 'politically incorrect' beliefs about black people and that relationship had taught Imani a valuable lesson about settling. She wasn't going to make the same mistake twice, especially when it was entirely preventable. Her attraction to Ajax had been explosive, but that didn't mean it was worth ignoring her common sense.

"You're quiet," Ajax said, smiling and turning towards her.

Seeing Ajax's perfect, strong body in front of her would make turning him down that much more difficult. Imani couldn't keep her eyes off his deep tan, his freckled chest and his bulging muscles. Ajax's arms were the thickest she'd ever seen and his chest was immaculately cut too. Just looking at him made her want him in her bed all over again.

"Yeah... I guess so."

"You know, this was real fun Imani... I'm wondering if there's a chance I can take you out... Like on a real date."

The phrase "real date" triggered Imani's "flight" response almost instantly. Secret, rough sex was one thing, but going on an actual date with Ajax threatened her commitment to herself to stay away from men, especially men who definitely had it in their power to hurt her.

"A... date?" Imani parroted back, trying to buy herself time.

"Sure... I mean... I don't want you to feel like I'm the type of guy who just takes a woman to bed when he has no interest in her."

Ajax's honesty made the fact that she had to reject him sting.

"Ajax, listen... I'm sorry," Imani started, "But I'm not interested in seeing anyone."

Ajax looked at her confused.

"I'm serious. I'm just looking for something casual and I just want to have fun."

Ajax stood up and stood before Imani fully nude.

"So you mean to say, you can just sleep with a guy and feel nothing?"

Imani bit down on her lip awkwardly. That wasn't the case at all. She did feel for Ajax, she just knew it wasn't realistic. She wasn't in any place to pursue a relationship and no matter how much she'd enjoyed a night with Ajax, she had to be pragmatic above all else.

Ajax asserted, "Okay. Then I really don't understand you. I'm outta here..."

"Ajax wait!" Imani called as he slipped into his boxers.

"What? You're looking for casual, I'll keep it casual."

His tone did a poor job at obscuring how wounded he felt.

"But you don't have to leave!?"

Ajax raised an eyebrow and kept his eyes on Imani for a moment. She wasn't sure what he was looking for, what emotions he was hoping to find beneath her abrasive surface. Imani looked back at him, her eyes exploring his face, trying to figure out his feelings too.

"You're a confusing woman, you know that? Is this what all city girls are like?"

"Confusing? How am I confusing?"

"No reason... I guess maybe I just read the signs you were putting out there all wrong. I'll stay. But just for tonight. Then I'll leave you alone missy, just like you want."

"Thanks," Imani said.

She knew it was foolish, but the moment Ajax had been so cool with them being "casual", she suddenly wanted him to fight for her. She suddenly wanted him to chase after her. Her primal desire to be pursued by her lover was activated in the worst way. Ajax climbed into bed next to her and Imani nuzzled close to him. She was embarrassed to admit it, but just this small intimacy felt restorative and healing.

The real reason she didn't want Ajax to leave was that she had no real desire to be alone, even if she didn't want to go out on a date with him. Her conflicting need for connection and her need to protect her heart left Imani in a confusing position. Ajax had no need to ask any more of her and he seemed content to hold her close.

"So, tell me about life in the big city," He said, "What's a girl like you doing out in Oklahoma without a sweet city gentleman to go home to..."

Imani bit down on her lower lip again. She didn't relish the idea of bringing up Brian to a complete stranger, but for Ajax to understand how confusing romance of any kind was to her, she'd have to mention Brian. He lay at the center of her anxiety about love. He was the man who had ripped Imani's heart into thousands of pieces and abandoned her just when she'd needed him most. Brian had never cared about her, and he'd made her doubt that anyone ever really could care about her.

"Lots of girls are single in the city. They say we're running out of men actually..."

Ajax laughed, "Yeah, but they aren't talking about beautiful women. It's only the ugly girls that are running out of men..."

"Ajax!" Imani said, playfully smacking him.

She sighed and continued, "Well fine, if you must know... I just got through a bad breakup."

Imani spent the rest of the night recounting her past with Brian, until she fell asleep in Ajax's arms, relieved that she could finally open up to someone. Ajax stayed awake for thirty minutes after Imani fell asleep. He watched her chest heaving up and down as she slept. He kept stroking her hair and her skin, occasionally planting kisses on her forehead until he was getting tired too.

Before Ajax slipped into sleep, he found himself wondering what kind of guy would hurt a sweet thing like Imani. She seemed high-strung, sure, but she had a soft and gentle heart that reminded him of his mother.

Morning Love

I n the morning, Imani felt the same reluctance towards Ajax, until she realized just how comfortable lying in his arms had been. She woke up for the first time in a long time, next to a man she felt safe with. Her ass pressed against Ajax's crotch and she could feel his morning wood poking through. He was fast asleep, snoring gently as if he were engaging in some sort of massive release of tension. Imani was just glad that she had nowhere specific to be in the morning.

Franco was waiting to hear back from the East Coast, and there wouldn't be any work for them to get started on until at least three in the afternoon. Imani could finally sleep in. She could finally experience the morning without the buzzing of her own mind propelling her anxiously forward from one task onto another. The only thing was, she couldn't move a muscle. Trapped underneath Ajax's strong, work man's arm, Imani found herself forced to be still.

Ajax grumbled and readjusted his warm body around hers. He nuzzled her hair and clutched her closely as if she were a teddy bear. Imani closed her eyes and tried to enjoy his presence fully. His body was so large, masculine and imposing. The magnetism Imani felt towards Ajax's physique was so primal. His body was tough, hardened by years of working outdoors. His skin possessed a deep, glowing tan. She wished she could have a repeat of the previous night. Unfortunately, she'd already kicked Ajax out the night before. The chances of him staying for the morning were incredibly low.

Imani's eyes snapped open again and she watched the sunlight pour in through a crack in her curtains. Ajax's blond arm hair stood up straight and he wriggled again. He would be awake soon and Imani knew she'd have to go through that awkward "morning after" song and dance with him.

She silently cussed herself under her breath for being so foolish as to ask him to stay over. If she wanted to have him gone, she should have just ripped the band-aid off and spent a night alone. Still, the protective warmth of Ajax's arms ensured Imani would have the best night's sleep of her life. Little Homer Oklahoma terrified her in so many ways. It was too small, too uniform, too country. But she'd found a sliver of pleasure here that she'd been unable to find on the East Coast. Something about the slow pace of the lazy days started to unwind Imani's deep-seeded tension.

Another sign of Ajax's waking appeared.

He began to kiss at her ears and nibble her lobes. Imani realized that he was awake and her wig was likely tilted unceremoniously to the side of her head, she began to panic over what Ajax would think once he completely awakened.

Imani tried to adjust the wig on her head as much as she possibly could. She was desperate to maintain the illusion that her beauty was 100% effortless.

"Good morning beautiful," Ajax whispered into her ears.

The hairs on the back of her neck stood up as his words brushed past the back of her neck on their way to her ears. The deep, masculine sound of Ajax's voice stirred a response between her legs.

"Good morning," Imani said.

Ajax rolled off of her, releasing her from his protective grasp and lying on his back.

"Um... Are you late for work?" Imani asked awkwardly.

He looked at her, wearing a smile across his face that told her the very pleasant memories of the night before were racing through his mind.

"Nope. Day off today. Well, until the afternoon. Then I gotta go help my paw."

"Lucky you."

"What about you? Don't you have to hustle on outta here and dig s'more dirt?"

Imani chuckled, "No. Need to wait for some lab results today so I'm free until the afternoon."

"Really?" Ajax asked, a mischievous look in his eye.

"Yup..."

Imani worried that he'd try to ask her out on a date again. She had the willpower to turn him down once, but she wasn't sure she could really deal with relentless requests.

"Then why don't we just stay here. I'll make you breakfast," Ajax said.

"You can cook?"

Ajax laughed in response.

"Of course I can cook! What, men don't cook out in the big fancy city? They do what? Order Chinese food?"

"I don't know," Imani replied.

"Well out here in the country, men can do it all sweetheart. We can cook, we can clean, we can milk cows and we can handle a woman in the bedroom..."

Imani figured he was right. At least he'd been right about the last part. Just the slightest thoughts of the previous night stimulated Imani's desires for more. She considered skipping the omelette and heading straight for an illicit dessert.

"Fine. You can make me breakfast then. And put on a pot of coffee while you're at it."

"Sassy... I like that in a woman."

Imani grinned. She got out of bed and made her way towards the shower.

"Let me just get cleaned up first..."

Imani turned the hot water on and stripped down to nothing. She rarely wore her natural hair out, but today she felt like going natural. She took off her wig and unbraided the cornrows that lay flat against her head. Imani's tough hair was begging for some moisture.

She got under the shower head and let the hot water saturate her tight, jet black coils. Her hair draped down to her shoulders, giving Imani some insight into what her hair's length would be without shrinkage. She massaged conditioner into her head and then lathered her body with black sulfur soap. Imani was obsessed with good skin care and sulfur soap had cleared up some of her stretch marks and blemishes, leaving her skin glowing.

When Imani was rinsing off in the shower, she suddenly heard the bathroom door bust open. The shower curtain flew open soon after. Ajax was standing before her totally naked, pointing his fully erect cock in her direction. Imani gasped when she saw him standing there, but Ajax didn't give her a second moment for further response.

"Turn around and bend over," He growled.

"Ajax!" She feigned an interest in protesting.

"Do what I said," He commanded.

Imani rested her arms against the wall and stuck her ass out. Thank goodness for a spacious hotel shower...

Ajax climbed into the shower behind her and started rubbing her lubricated body up and down. With his cock pressing into her ass, he pinched Imani's nipples. She emitted a soft moan as he began to massage the flesh of her hanging breasts. Ajax stroked her nipples and then pinched them lightly.

He took his hands and began to rub Imani's body, allowing his hand to rest on her ass cheeks and squeeze them tightly.

"Mmmm," She moaned as his hand darted to her pussy lips for the first time.

Feeling Ajax's dominating and imposing frame behind her activated Imani's desires in a big way. She stuck her ass out further and wriggled it, trying to get him to skip the foreplay and ease his member as deep into her as it could go.

"Please," Imani implored.

She couldn't finish the sentence she wanted to finish as Ajax slipped his fingers between her pussy lips and began to massage the hardened nub between her legs. Imani braced herself against the wall and then emitted a loud moan as Ajax's touch engorged her clit.

"More..." Imani moaned breathily.

Ajax started to massage her clit in slow, smooth circles. Imani ignored her knees desire to buckle beneath her as he coaxed her towards a powerful climax. Imani thrust her hips back to allow Ajax greater access to her wetness. Hot water poured over them and ran down her back in steamy rivulets, adding to the erotic sensations stimulated by Ajax's touch.

She could feel his hard cock pressing into her ass, almost more eager than she was to enter her and make sweet love.

Imani reached a loud release. She groaned and pushed her hips back as her pussy contracted and fluids flowed from her pussy. Now, Ajax was finally ready to enter her. Imani looked back and pointed him towards her emergency rubbers. Ajax rolled a condom onto his hardness and then pushed Imani's head so it was looking away from him.

Even more wetness pooled between her thighs as he exercised the smallest bit of dominance. Imani loved how in control Ajax was. She loved how he could mix his power with protective energy that made her feel submissive without feeling used. Ajax spread her legs apart even further and then began to press his cock into her pussy from behind.

He gripped Imani's protruding ass cheeks as he started to squeeze his thick, long cock into her. Imani moaned as she felt Ajax's bulging head fit past her tight entrance. She continued to brace herself against the wall as Ajax thrust another few inches inside her. The angle of his cock grazed her g-spot ever so gently, subjecting Imani to a strong surge of pleasure.

Imani gasped as Ajax lodged his full length between her pussy. The sensation of his hardness stretching out her pussy and grazing her juicy outer lips. Ajax held onto Imani's hips and began to thrust into her forcefully. His quick, deep thrusts revealed the intensity of Ajax's hunger for Imani.

With each deep stroke, she felt Ajax's dick touching deeper and deeper into her pussy. Imani grunted and pushed her hips back to meet his thrusts. She was dripping wet and enjoying the primal, urgent nature of Ajax's hard pounding. He squeezed her ass cheeks tighter and pulled them apart, watching Imani's tight asshole as he pounded away at her pussy.

He was tempted to take her forbidden hole, but not yet...

He could feel Imani's breathing grow more and more shallow as she approached climax. Ajax slowed down his thrusts so he could reach in front of Imani and access her wetness. Imani groaned loudly at the combination of Ajax's fingers pressed against her clit and his cock fully embedded in her pussy.

"Yes... Take me... Take me daddy," She moaned.

Imani's naughty words of encouragement egged Ajax on. He began to thrust into her harder and harder as he rubbed her clit to another climax. Imani exclaimed loudly as she came again. She could feel Ajax slowing down too as he approached a climax of his own. Her skin felt hot and rejuvenated from the time under the hot water and the urgent thrusting between her legs.

"Ohhh! Yes!" Imani exclaimed as she climaxed again.

Ajax grunted and his cock twitched between

Imani's legs as he released hefty spurts of semen. He slowly eased his dick out from between Imani's legs and disposed of the condom. Imani turned around, her legs quivering from the intense love-making she'd just experienced. But Ajax was no longer in the bathroom.

"That... was... so... hot..." Imani whispered to herself.

She finished up her shower with a big smile on her face. Out of the shower, she massaged jojoba oil and almond oil into her hair and then applied lotion to every inch of her skin. Imani emerged from the shower with a white plush bathrobe wrapped around her body.

"Good shower?" Ajax asked as he stood at Imani's stove in just his boxers, tending something cooking in the skillet.

"A very... very... good shower."

"Good. It would be a shame if some rogue got in there with you and mussed things up."

Imani just smiled. Her mind was wandering to the sexual encounter she'd finished just seconds before. Ajax's hands wandering all over her body. Reaching orgasm with her body pressed against the walls of the shower. Ajax's hands touching her in the most exquisite places. If this was what Ajax had in mind for a relaxing morning, Imani could get behind it.

Ajax served them bacon, eggs and toast. Imani was stunned by how well he'd prepared anything. Brian had always insisted that bacon could be cooked "medium-rare" (it couldn't) and that fried eggs were better with "a little yolk" (he ate them practically raw).

"This is delicious..."

"Well it ain't a luxury breakfast, but I figured I'd work with what I have."

They ate quietly for a few minutes until Imani noticed Ajax's eyes boring into her.

"What?" She asked.

"Huh?"

"You're staring."

"Oh," Ajax replied.

He didn't confirm or deny whether or not he was staring and he didn't seem too eager to reveal why.

"Why? What are you looking it?"

"Just you... You're beautiful Imani. I have so many questions about you, that's all."

Imani looked down shyly. She understood that Ajax had a lot on his mind when it came to her, but she wasn't sure how much further she could let him in. She'd already slept with him more times than she'd intended to. She'd already told him her entire history with Brian — every sordid detail from their broken engagement to his unending infidelity.

Imani hoped that she hadn't given Ajax the wrong impression. She didn't want to be fixed. She didn't want to be saved. And even if she did, Oklahoma wasn't exactly where she'd go if she were looking for love. Her trip out west would be short. Not enough time to fall in love, or even get to know someone.

"What kind of questions do you have?"

"Well... I want to know why you're so scared to go out on a silly date."

"I'm not scared!" Imani asserted.

Ajax grinned, "Yes you are. And I don't think it's 'cause of your ex either. It's just one date Imani, not a marriage proposal."

"Will you just drop it Ajax?"

"Maybe," He said, a mischievous glint in his eye.

Imani didn't know why she found herself so drawn to a man who could be such a pain in the butt. In many ways, Ajax refused to take "no" for an answer. He was always probing, always curious, always trying to "figure her out".

"Well, there's nothing for you to figure out. I'm a simple gal, who's sworn off men."

"Oh?" Ajax said, his lips twitched as he teetered on the verge of laughter.

"Yes... Yes daddy," He moaned, imitating Imani's words in the shower.

"Ajax, stop!" Imani huffed.

Ajax let out a loud laugh — giving Imani an auditory sense of what the word "guffaw" really meant. She was annoyed with him, but she still couldn't softening up at the sound of his laugh. He might have been irritating her, but he meant well.

"C'mon, I didn't mean it like that. I'm just teasing."

"Well, if you've got a problem with how I sound, you don't have to sleep with me."

Ajax's face softened.

"Imani, I didn't mean it like that. I'm just saying... your hiatus from men seems to be highly contextual."

"Maybe it is," Imani said stiffly, "Maybe men are only good for sex."

Ajax chuckled again. Imani couldn't figure out why he seemed to think everything that she said was so gosh darn funny.

"You don't believe that Imani Raymond. I know you don't believe that."

Imani finished her breakfast with a grim expression on her face. She didn't want to dignify Ajax's assertion with a response. He took far too much pleasure in torturing her. Once they'd eaten, Ajax seemed hell bent on leading her to the hotel room bed again. He clutched at Imani's flesh as they lay in bed together.

At first, he teased her slowly. He whispered all the ways he wanted to make love to her in her ear until she was dripping wet. Then he stuck his hands between her thighs and collected some of the sticky fluid that had pooled there. He tasted her, and made her watch. Then, he made her taste herself. Imani's pussy was crying out for another pounding. But she didn't want to beg — wouldn't that be classified as sending mixed messages?

Ajax untied Imani's bathrobe and positioned his muscled, masculine physique on top of her. He was hard again. He seemed to have the stamina and eagerness of a teenager. His love of sex was something Imani shared — even if her desires had been buried beneath other priorities like her PhD, her hunt for a husband and even sometimes mundane tasks like laundry or doing the dishes.

"Beg for it," Ajax whispered into her ears.

Imani refused to beg. She wouldn't let him have the upper hand here. She'd told him exactly what she didn't want and the last thing Imani planned to do was muddy the waters between her and this cowboy who couldn't seem to take no for an answer.

But the teasing. Oh, the teasing. His fingers

grazed her pussy lips ever so close to her clit. But he refused to actually touch her. She mewled and she whimpered but all he would do was stroke around her wetness as she did so. Ajax refused to budge until she begged. Then she had to fight against his kisses. His hot mouth pressed against her neck, taking her flesh as deep as he could. Imani's moans did nothing to stir Ajax.

In a test of stubbornness, Imani knew she might very well lose, whether she wanted to admit it or not. With Ajax's lips against her neck and his hand dangerously close to her clit, she would have to give in. Before that last resort, Imani bucked her hips upward, trying to trick Ajax's hand into diving between her folds and giving her release. No such ploy would work.

"I said to beg, Imani..." He growled into her ear.

His primal growling into her ear weakened her resolve not to give into him. Through her heavy breathing, Imani finally managed to whimper, "Please..."

A smirk slipped onto Ajax's face. He seemed relieved to finally allow himself to give into her desires. Which were really their desires. His fingers found her clit and he began to rub Imani's wetness in steady circles. She couldn't hold back much longer. Without even feeling Ajax's hardness pressed into her again, Imani climaxed. Her legs quivered and trembled. Her body convulsed as pleasure took over every inch of her flesh.

What right did Ajax have to possess this effect on her? He pressed his lips to her neck again, causing her vibrating against the bed to continue more. He slipped a condom onto his cock again and spread her legs wide.

"You're so wet... so tight and wet..." He muttered.

Imani reached for his cock in an attempt to pull him closer and force him to release inside her. He dodged her hand and forced his own tender pace. Ajax's hardness edged closer to Imani as she gasped.

"Beg for it again," He growled.

She knew better this time than to toy with him. She was learning the lesson that when Ajax wanted something, he wouldn't give in. When it came to sex, he was clearly a hunter. He'd bent her over in the shower and pounded her like lust had sent him crazy. And now, he had a fierce look in his cobalt eyes that told her the same man was approaching her again.

She begged.

"Please... Give me your cock... Stick your big hard cock inside me," Imani allowed the dirty words to flow out of her mouth.

Ajax slipped his thick cock into her in one swift

motion. Imani cried out from the pain of being entered by such a massively large force. He stretched her out instantly and then began to pound away without allowing Imani a moment to readjust to being penetrated by his enormous dick. She grabbed Ajax's ass cheeks and squeezed them tightly as he thrust into her.

The headboard banged against the wall like a devilish symphony of lust. With each thrust, Imani felt her moans growing louder and louder. Franco wasn't her only likely audience this time. But Imani didn't care. She dug her nails into Ajax's back as he pressed his hardness deeper and faster. His eyes were burning with ferocious desire.

Imani's face twisted into primal pleasure as she climaxed. Her pussy gripped Ajax's hardness tighter and he plunged into her as fast as he could go. She was dripping, soaking wet and still craving more. She could lie like this for hours, just allowing Ajax to use her tightness as a sleeve for his massive cock.

"Yes... Yes... Harder..." Imani begged.

Ajax was more than happy to oblige. He continued to pummel Imani's pussy, feeling his balls tighten close to his body, he knew he didn't have much longer to enjoy the reserved woman's sopping cunt. He pressed his lips to hers again as he drove deeper into her. He felt her warm body writhe beneath him as she came again. He silenced her screams with his lips and pounded her hard. He felt his cock stiffening but didn't slow down the pace one bit.

His skin prickled into gooseflesh but he continued to stare into her deep brown eyes and thrust into her. Her pussy was so hot... So... tight...

Ajax grunted loudly and then came. The twitching of his cock between Imani's legs triggered another earth-shattering orgasm. They lay in each other's arms shuddering and quivering with unspeakable pleasure. Sex had never felt this way to either of them ever before. With each climax, they transformed.

When Ajax rolled over onto his back, Imani wove her fingers through his instinctively. She didn't think of it as breaching the boundaries she'd intentionally set between them. They'd just made love in the most connected way and her body, against her will, was pursuing that connection with full ferocity.

"So... This afternoon... You're headed towards my paw's ranch right?"

Imani nodded.

"Well. I'm sure it will be a trip... I think he wanted me over there."

"Well," Imani said, startled, "We should definitely arrive separately."

Ajax chuckled, "You think there's any pretense between you and your partner about us?"

Imani bit down on her lower lip thinking about the loud moaning and the banging headboard against the paper-thin hotel room walls. Even if it was a "fancy" suite, this place was hardly soundproof.

"It's not about that," Imani asserted, "It's just... It wouldn't look right."

"Like an environmental conflict of interest?"

"Something like that."

Imani wasn't interested in having a discussion about this. Having Ajax in her bedroom was one thing, parading him around in public was another entirely. It just wasn't what she wanted right now. Life was complicated enough and Imani knew that she should be focusing on work, especially during work hours.

"Well, why don't I get out of your hair ma'am," Ajax said.

He rolled out of bed. Imani watched Ajax's robust back tense up as he started to dress. Imani couldn't get enough of his physique. She watched him slip into the previous night's clothes and then Ajax planted a kiss on her forehead before leaving. There was no talk of seeing Imani again. She wasn't sure whether or not she wanted to see Ajax.

Around an hour after Ajax left, Franco knocked on Imani's door. She wasn't sure if he was going to chastise her for her loud romp the previous night or grill her about the suave cowboy she'd taken into her bedroom. Franco said nothing. He answered the door with a smirk, but that was it. With results back from New York, he couldn't bother himself with the trivialities of Imani's sex life.

"What do we have then?" Imani asked.

Franco held up his phone and began to read the message from their director out loud. Apparently, the soil tests had been inconclusive. There was damage, but it was hard to determine where the damage had come from. They'd need a clearer picture of the ranch's pesticide usage on the Redford Ranches as well as a better picture of the history of the crops on the ranch — of which there weren't many in the first place.

"There's also some suggestion that if there is any pollution, it might be intentional."

"Intentional?"

Imani felt chills run down her spine as she entertained the notion that Ajax (in conjunction with his father, or on his own) could possibly be involved in some kind of scheme. It would have to be for insurance or something. Could it be possible that the man who could make her see stars could also have dark greed pulsing beneath his skin.

Imani pursed her lips and folded her arms, waiting for Franco's response.

"Hey, it's nothing yet. This is just a cursory investigation. But if there's any type of illegal anything going on, we'll need to find out."

"But we aren't the police!"

"I know. But if we keep our heads down, see any evidence of anything, we'll have to go to the police."

Imani nodded.

"Well, we'd better head over to Redford Ranch number two," Imani said.

"Yup. You'll get to meet your tasty little cowboy's daddy."

"Gross," Imani muttered.

Franco chuckled at his own joke as they both eased into their jackets. Imani thought about what could possibly be going on in this small town. There was something chilling about how benign Homer, Oklahoma seemed on the surface. It was as if nothing could be so perfect and pristine. The corn had no right to exude such a brilliant green. The sky had no right to be so blue.

They got into their car. Franco drove, as usual, and they made their way to Redford Ranch. Imani felt increasingly nervous as they drove closer. She'd be seeing Ajax again and she wanted to keep the fact that they had made-love secret. She already felt like she was wearing a scarlet letter on her chest. Only a short time in Oklahoma and she'd already fallen into bed with Ajax. It wasn't something Imani was proud of, even if she had to admit to herself every minute of Ajax had been incredible.

Still, their attraction was a private matter. As private as such matters could be in small-town motels with paper-thin walls. Imani wondered if Ajax's father would be anything like him. While she'd talked endlessly about herself, she had to admit that she didn't know very much about the blond hunk who she'd hopped into bed with the night before.

Their car pulled into a lot and Imani and Franco were faced with a ranch even bigger than the first one. Lester Redford was clearly rolling in dough. For a small town Oklahoma man, he owned so much land, he could probably sustain the Redford family line for generations. Having two of the biggest ranches in town probably meant that everyone in Homer knew Ajax's face and name quite well.

"Feel a bit uneasy here... I bet the father's nothing like his son," Franco said nervously.

Imani didn't reply, but she felt the same anxiety that Franco did. They got out of the car and walked towards the door of the ranch house. They were expected here, Franco had called Lester Redford himself to ensure it would be alright to show up on his land. He seemed like the kind of guy to have guns — plenty of 'em — and Franco wanted to be prepared.

Before Franco could knock on the door, a man opened it. The first thing that struck Imani was Lester's striking resemblance to his son. If his son were older and a bit less handsome. His eyes were a bright cornflower blue and sunken into his head. Lester's forehead protruded forward; Imani could imagine that as a young man, his hairline had disguised his forehead's peculiar jut. His teeth were crooked and a few were missing. He smelled like cigars and mulch.

"Y'all them scientists, right?"

"Yes sir, may we come in for a moment? We have a few questions we'd like to ask you."

"Eh," Lester grunted, moving out of the house instead of letting them in.

"Let's walk 'round 'ere 'nstead," He mumbled.

As he walked out of the house, he pulled a pack of cigarettes out of the back of his pocket.

"Need a smoke?"

Franco and Imani declined. Lester let out a chilling laugh.

"Y'all b'lieve these gov'mint lies 'bout tobacco killin' ya?"

He lit up and took a long drag. Imani could tell that Franco was tempted, but too focused on the science to accept Lester's offer. Lester started walking. Both Franco and Imani figured that they'd better follow him. Imani spied a tractor in the distance and she knew instinctively it was Ajax. She found odd comfort in the fact that he was close by.

"Now... What d'y'all need to know," Lester grunted.

He eyed Imani with a strange look that seemed like he was trying to quell his disgust. Imani couldn't bear to look him in the eye. She'd leave that difficult job up to Franco.

Something about Lester made her blood run cold. Considering how easy-going she felt around his son, Imani wasn't expecting a physiological response like this. Each time she looked at Lester's face, she felt a lump forming in her throat. Her primal fear response seemed to be trying to warn her of something that she couldn't quite place.

Now, she was just listening for any kind of evidence that they'd find something worth exploring on the Redford Ranch. It wouldn't do to have nothing to report back to base. For a guy with two ranches in Homer alone, Lester seemed shockingly humble. Imani wondered if this was genuinely the case or if Lester wanted to project a particular innocent image out into the world.

Franco asked Lester Redford about pesticide usage, waste dumping and a number of mundane questions. Lester had no trouble answering each one without a hint of nervousness that might have betrayed a lie. He seemed scary, but honest. He peppered each of his statements with a side lecture about the current "demon" that had been "sent from Africa" to ruin "American values".

Every time he mentioned "Africa", he shot Imani a dirty look. Imani was sure she hadn't imagined the looks of disdain. She'd been black long enough to recognize when she was in the same space as a bigot — someone who had no reason to hate her, but hated her anyways from the very bottom of their core. Perhaps that had been the root of her discomfort around Lester. She'd just been able to tell what kind of man he was.

Imani found herself tuning out, allowing herself to push the rage and frustration deep inside her. But in tuning out, Imani stopped hearing anything Lester had to say. Franco would have to analyze it all later and catch her up on what she'd missed — at least the parts that had nothing to do with conspiracy theories.

Imani's eyes wandered out to Ajax's tractor out in the field. How could a man like Ajax, who seemed so good at his core, be bred from a man like Lester who seemed to spew hate and tobacco smoke at the same rate.

As Imani's mind wandered, she failed to notice the terrain getting rockier. Before she could catch herself, she missed her step and started to tumble down a small hill.

"Imani! Be careful!" Franco's voice came too late.

Imani thought she felt or heard an impact.

Then, lights out.

Heart of Darkness

Dull throbbing. Then the smell of old, damp wood. The smell began to choke her and as Imani gasped for a clean breath of air, she came to. Her body felt tired — the way one's body felt tired after a long, hard run. She tried to open her eyes but they were still heavy. The dull throbbing on the side of Imani's head worsened each time she tried to move.

Her toes broke free from the pain first. Imani wriggled her toes and realized that someone had taken her shoes off, and her socks. Her eyes fluttered open but darting them around the room too much strained her muscles and sent pain shooting through her skull.

After a few moments awake, she guessed that

she'd somehow ended up in inside Lester Redford's ranch house. That would explain the muted scent of mulch that permeated the room. Imani could hear muffled voices talking downstairs. One of them had to be Lester and then of course, she heard Franco's booming voice.

The last thing Imani remembered was walking around the ranch. Based on the pain in her head, she must have fallen somehow and whacked herself in the head. Ouch. Imani breathed slowly and tried to move her legs off the bed. Moving her head still hurt. She wasn't sure if she had a concussion or not. If she did, it was probably mild since the light in the bedroom caused very little irritation.

The soreness was all over her body. Imani tried to see if she could spy any bruises from her position, but she couldn't see a thing without sitting up.

After five minutes of shifting and shuffling in bed, she finally managed to sit up. Imani doubled over, planting her forearms on her thighs. Nausea rumbled inside her stomach as she moved. The whack to her head had obviously been very hard. They'd left her here to rest in lieu of easy access to a physician. The doctor only came into town once a week and other than that, he was a forty minute drive out of Homer.

The middle of nowhere indeed. Visits to the doctor were restricted to absolute emergencies.

Imani raised her head and took a good look around the bedroom. The smell probably came from the fact that it was an unused guest room. Or maybe it had been Ajax's room at one point. She knew that Ajax lived down at the other Redford ranch in town, so if this were his bedroom, it might have been so a long time ago.

The bed was made up with cream colored sheets that smelled both clean and musty at the same time. Dust had settled on them from months (or perhaps years) of going unused. The walls were covered in an old, 70s style floral wallpaper and the dark, hard-wood closet doors pulled the room's mismatched, rustic style together in a bizarre way.

The talking downstairs was still going on and Imani wondered if she should use this opportunity to take a look around. From the moment she'd laid eyes on him, Lester had given Imani the creeps. It wasn't just his rants about the government, it was something else. Some fears were so deep and primal that they didn't require explanation, and almost seemed to shun reason.

Imani stood up, the dust from the floorboards collected around her toes. She wiped her feet off on the carpet and tested the boards for creaks before she made her way to the nightstand near the bed. She opened the top drawer as quietly as possible. There was nothing there of any import — just a small, tattered bible and a few empty bullet casings.

Imani opened the Bible and saw the inscription on the front cover.

"MARIE REDFORD — 1977."

MARIE. The name didn't ring a bell, but Imani guessed that it was Ajax's mother. He'd never brought her up and Imani hadn't noticed any woman around either of Lester Redford's ranches. Maybe she'd passed away. Still testing the floorboards to ensure that they wouldn't betray her, Imani moved towards an old chest of drawers.

Sitting on top of the chest of drawers was a vase with a single fake flower in it. That was probably Lester's idea of decor. Then there was a full box of cigarette's — Pall Mall's — and a lighter. Imani opened the top drawer and saw a stack of old documents written with a type writer. She rifled through them quickly and saw nothing interesting. A few titles for horses that Lester had bought at the turn of the new millennium.

Then, there was a letter from the Homer sheriff regarding a barn raising in the next town over. There were a few letters from school regarding Lester's son Ajax and "bad behavior".

Imani smirked as she saw them. It was hard for her to imagine what Ajax might have been like as a little boy. They hadn't exactly done much talking about his childhood. It was strange how Imani felt like she knew him so well already. Their communication had transcended words and their connection wasn't something she knew, it was something she'd felt.

Imani moved to the new drawer down. Something in the back of her mind was propelling her forward, even if she had no clue what she was looking for. There had been nothing explicitly suspicious about either Lester or Ajax. And Imani already knew her mind was biased in favor of Ajax's innocence (for a number of reasons). Still, she pressed on towards another drawer.

The second drawer on the bureau was far more interesting. Imani came across a small shoebox labeled "Ajax". The handwriting was scrappy but legible. The box looked old and unbothered. Imani waited and listened for noises coming from downstairs.

She heard Franco's voice say "...outside..." and then she heard the front door close. They probably presumed that she was asleep still. Imani realized that no matter what, she couldn't have been unconscious for that long. Maybe fifteen minutes. And now, they were leaving her to rest, and she was going to find any dirty laundry that the Redford's might have hidden on their ranch.

Imani suspected if she found any dirty laundry, it would be Lester's. Compared to his son, Lester Redford was just sinister.

Imani took the cover off the box and saw a few returned letters that Ajax had addressed to Marie Redford. Apparently, she was out in Omaha, Nebraska. Or she had been. Since the letters had been returned, Imani presumed Ajax's mother never received them. Something complicated had gone on with Ajax, Lester and his mother. Imani wondered briefly what it was. There were no other signs that either of the ranches had a womanly touch to them; if she'd been gone, she'd been gone a long time.

The rest of the papers in the box were old love letters from high-school sweethearts. A prom photo of Ajax standing next to a thin blonde girl with mismatched blonde extensions, an aqua blue dress and cowboy boots. Imani couldn't help but smile. Prom out west was very different from anything in New York. She couldn't imagine what the mean girls at her high school would have said about a girl wearing cowboy boots to the prom.

The box yielded nothing. Imani replaced it in the drawer just as she found it and moved to the final drawer in the bureau.

The final drawer was empty. There was one folded, hand-woven blanket that looked like a Native American design of some kind. Imani closed the drawer and tip-toed to the window. Franco was crouched close to the ground, hands over his eyes looking out towards the horizon. Lester was smoking and Ajax was standing next to them both, silent with his lips pursed.

Looking out at Ajax from above, Imani confirmed in her mind how attractive he was. She'd been with good looking guys before, but not men like Ajax. He was in a class of his own — the class of sexy that propelled her to make silly decisions just because her heart fluttered a few times.

Imani wondered what Franco had managed to stir out of Lester — and if he'd become more amenable now that he wasn't talking to a black woman.

Imani faced the tall, dark-wood wardrobe. It

seemed to stare at her ominously, as if behind the doors there was some sort of ghost, waiting to jump out at her. Imani took a deep breath and pulled the doors open.

The scent of damp wood filled the room even more. There were two old tweed suits suspended from flimsy wire hangers. Then, there was a black vinyl bag with a zipper down the front suspended from a similar hanger. Beneath it, there was a brown, wooden box. Imani reached out for the suit bag and pulled it out.

She pulled the zipper down in one swift motion and recoiled the instant she saw what was inside. The white on the robe had faded to the point where it was almost beige. Right above the breast was the klan insignia that had inspired terror in many for generations. The white, pointed hood hung back behind the robes. Imani felt her breath getting short.

She dropped the hanger to the ground and prayed that it hadn't made a loud noise.

Klan robes. She'd actually laid hands on the robes of a member of the Ku Klux Klan. She was in his house, right in the pit with the viper. Imani heard the front door open. She picked the hanger up off of the ground, threw the zipper up quickly and replaced the robes in the cupboard.

The bottom step creaked.

She closed the wardrobe doors.

Another step creaked. Franco's voice spilled under the door, "I hope she's resting."

Imani flopped into bed and closed her eyes. Her heart was racing so fast, she wasn't sure if she could pull off pretending to be a sleep. The door thrust open and Ajax, Franco and Lester stood in the doorway.

"Imani?" Franco called.

"Mm?" Imani mumbled, opening her eyes.

When she looked at Lester, it was like he had changed. Imani knew logically that he hadn't, but her discovery gave him a more evil look. His blue eyes suddenly seemed to be tinted with darkness. The smoke billowing from his lips was a definite sign of fire.

"She's awake, thank goodness."

"I'll have to take her to the doctor if she's still bad tomorrow," Franco said.

He moved towards Imani's bed and sat at the foot.

"Does it hurt?" He asked.

Imani sat up slowly. The throbbing in her head had returned, but it was less painful than when she'd first woken up. She intentionally avoided eye contact with Ajax.

"It hurts a bit."

"Maybe we should get her some ice?" Ajax offered, pushing past Lester who replied in a low grunt.

Imani looked at Ajax with a mixture of bewilderment and confusion. Ajax. She wanted to trust him, but how could she after what she'd found. Sure, fathers and sons could be different, but how different could they really be? Ajax had grown up alone with a literal klansman for a father. Just the thought of it seemed like it was some kind of horror story.

Imani was no fool. She knew racists existed in the East Coast as well, but at least in the circles she ran in, they obscured their prejudice. They didn't hang it proudly in the closet like a badge of honor. She recoiled from Ajax's touch as he tried to feel for a bump on her head where she fell.

"Easy. Just seeing if there's a bump."

There wasn't. Ajax's hand slithered along her skull like a snake. Was he wearing a mask? Or was he really the caring guy she thought he was? Imani looked at Franco, hoping she could urge him to leave with a glance.

"She seems fine," Franco said, "Thanks for the spare bed Mr. Redford. We'll be coming back with some more questions later this week if you don't mind."

Lester shrugged, but didn't reply verbally. Franco helped Imani out of bed.

"Shoes?" She asked.

Ajax chimed in, "I took 'em off you and set 'em at the door."

Imani didn't acknowledge him or make eye contact with him. She could handle a lot of things — what she couldn't handle was the thought that she might have gotten into bed with a hot-blooded racist. With her head pounding, avoidance was the only weapon in her arsenal.

She rested her weight on Franco. Taking bigger steps took a lot out of her. Franco walked her past Lester and Ajax. They took the stairs slowly. Lester lit another cigarette before they arrived at the bottom step. Ajax was doing a bad job of "playing it cool". Imani could feel his eyes boring into her, wondering what was wrong. She didn't know if she could ever find it in her heart to tell him.

Franco led her to a chair and he helped slide her socks and shoes onto her feet. Imani's head started to spin. Walking down the stairs had been a challenge. She silently cursed herself for being so silly as to take such a big fall. If she'd been paying attention, this would have never happened.

"Are you taking me to the doctor?" Imani asked.

Franco shook his head.

"If your head hurts tomorrow we'll go, alright?"

Imani nodded, wincing as her head moved up and down. She leaned on Franco as they walked out of the house. Lester grunted good bye and turned his back on them the moment they were out of the door. As they were close to the car, Ajax burst out of the ranch house and walked quickly towards Imani.

"Imani! Wait!" Franco walked around Imani to the driver's side.

She folded her arms as Ajax approached her. Imani didn't exactly think it was "subtle" to run up to her like that in front of Ajax and within view of his father.

"Yes...?" She asked, trying to sound calmer than she felt.

"Everything alright?"

Imani shrugged, "I just hit my head..."

"That ain't what I mean."

"I don't know what you mean then."

"Can I see you?"

"I don't know if that's a good idea... My head..."

"Right. Sure. And nothing happened that's making you so cold right now?"

"I'm not cold," Imani defended herself but she could see that Ajax didn't believe her.

Was she supposed to tell him what she'd found?

"Alright. Well I'll just leave you be then."

Imani detected the soreness in his voice, but there was nothing she could do about it — nothing she wanted to do about it while Franco was standing right there at least. Ajax opened her car door and Imani slipped in. He closed the door and then stormed off without saying goodbye.

"Trouble in paradise?" Franco asked with a smirk.

"Shut up," Imani grumbled, resting her head back in the passenger seat.

Franco chuckled and then pulled the car off the lot. Imani knew there would be no keeping this from Franco, but she wasn't exactly eager to talk to him about it. He'd get on his "I told you so" high horse.

"So... What happened?"

"You fell. Pretty bad. You were out for a while. Your boy toy and I carried you upstairs and I continued investigating."

"He's not my boy toy," Imani snapped.

Franco smirked.

"Something's off about that Lester guy, but I don't know what. He doesn't seem too interested in the fact that his ranches might be experiencing devastating levels of pollution... It's odd."

"Maybe he caused the pollution," Imani shrugged.

"Maybe... But it's still odd. He's closed off but

there's no reason to be. I get that we're government snakes, but we're supposed to be helping this community."

Imani didn't reply. She watched the infinite rows of corn and silently wondered if this town deserved their help. She wondered if she should tell Franco about what she'd discovered. She hated keeping things from him. Only, this wasn't relevant to work — only relevant to her feelings about Ajax. If there were still any feelings left. The knock to Imani's head had made her cynical (at least for the day).

"Well, we just have to keep researching. If he doesn't want our help, we'll deal with other ranchers in Homer. We have time here."

"Maybe too much time," Franco grumbled.

"What? Getting sick of the fact that you can't go clubbing?" Imani teased.

"Easy for you to say, you already have a tasty cowboy doing your bidding."

Imani huffed, "He's not 'mine'."

"That's not what I heard last night."

Imani stared out the window without responding to him.

"Oh come on Imani, don't get all pissy. You know I think it's a good thing. You deserve to have some fun after Brian."

"Well... That's all it is. Fun."

"Sure, of course. Listen, I know we're here for work but we're also close friends. If you want to get involved in extracurriculars, no one has to know. As long as you aren't sponsoring him on the government's dime."

Imani smiled. The idea of a rich rancher's son being sponsored by her amused her, just as Franco knew it would.

"You're something else, you know that?"

Franco didn't say a word as they pulled into the motel parking lot. When she went upstairs to her bedroom, Imani's head started to feel a little better. Franco insisted that she take the next day off — he'd repeat what they'd done at the Redford's on the other ranches. Imani considered protesting, but she knew deep down that she needed the time off.

Her blood ran cold as she recalled what she'd found in Lester Rutherford's cupboard. She'd never actually seen Klan robes up close. She knew what they looked like from history classes. And she had heard rumors that the Klan was still active, that it wasn't a thing of the past. Still, Imani had no reason to believe those rumors were anything other than a mythology. Progress was coming slowly, right? Racism was dying, and Klan members were old, wheezing nobodies.

That's what she'd believed anyhow.

Alone in her room, Imani dimmed the lights and shut the curtains. She locked the door and stripped down to nothing before climbing into bed. The throbbing in her head had mostly subsided but she took a couple more painkillers anyways. She still didn't remember the details of the fall.

Imani got into bed and didn't bother flicking on the TV or straining her eyes with a book. She just closed her eyes and slipped quickly away into darkness.

When Imani woke up in the morning, the pain in her head was gone. She didn't even feel dizzy, or any of the other signs that might have suggested she had a concussion. It was early still, judging by the position of the sun in the sky. Franco probably hadn't left for work yet.

Imani walked into their shared space and saw Franco over by the coffee maker in his work pants and a white tee.

"Headache?" He asked.

Imani shook her head.

"Good. you conked out early so I bet that helped you heal right up. Lemme see."

He gestured for Imani to come closer and she did, allowing Franco to feel her skull for bumps or bruises. There were none.

"Looks like we can skip the trek to the doctor today."

"Yeah."

"I still think you have no business in the field. One day off won't kill you. Plus, there's no rule saying we can't enjoy our time out here."

That was one of the perks of being an environmental scientist like they were. As long as you produced results, the boss didn't care if you spent half the day hiking with your head in the clouds, searching for a rare bird or whatever had caught your eye. Imani appreciated the flexibility in the field; it made up for the high tension and stress in the office.

"The rest will be good for me."

"Want breakfast?"

Imani nodded. Franco toasted bagels for both of them and got out the prosciutto and cream cheese. The bagels out here were dry compared to the ones in New York, but Imani was too hungry to protest. She'd been so exhausted that she'd forgotten dinner the night before. After wolfing down two bagels and two mugs of extra-creamy coffee, Imani started to feel full.

Franco got ready for work, and then left her alone. Imani started off her morning by taking a shower. She dressed in a warm blouse and pencil skirt, even if she was just staying at the motel, and she affixed a shoulder length wig to her head. Imani didn't bother applying much makeup before returning to her room.

She pulled out the paperback she'd brought along with her for entertainment and curled up in her chair. Imani felt more nervous being here alone than she'd ever felt in the most dangerous parts of New York. She felt disgusted with what she'd seen, but even more than that, she felt disgusted with herself for getting duped by Ajax.

The more she thought about it, the more she couldn't deny the fact that Ajax had to share at least some of his father's beliefs. You didn't grow up with a parent who wanted the extermination of black folk and end up a warrior against racism. Imani hated to be cynical, but it was just common knowledge that people ended up just like their parents. Imani felt disgusted with herself for falling for his wily seduction, for allowing him into her bed, for even entertaining the idea that they could have any type of relationship with each other, casual or otherwise.

The twisted ideas of what Ajax might really have thought about her turned Imani's mind sour. Focusing on the pages in front of her became a challenge.

After she'd re-read the same paragraph ten

times over, Imani heard a loud thudding knock against her door. Must be room service ignoring the "Do Not Disturb" sign. Imani stood up and hastened towards the peep hole. No room service. Just Ajax.

Imani tried to tiptoe back from the door but Ajax called out, "I know you're there Imani. I saw Franco's car speedin' down Main Street."

Crap. There was no way out. She could either face him now or later. At least today, she'd have the day off to deal with whatever aftermath came from this.

Imani opened the door with a stubborn look on her face that cautioned Ajax against crossing her. Ajax looked at her with a wide smile on his face. His blond hair was slicked back and his eyes were shining bright with excitement.

"What's gotten into you? I came to check on you Imani."

"Thanks. I'm doing fine," She replied curtly. Too curtly to go unnoticed.

Ajax raised an eyebrow.

"Gonna let me in?"

Imani sighed, "Sure."

She let Ajax in and then moved to her chair, sitting quietly.

"Head still hurt?"

"It's better this morning."

"I swear... Something's different Imani... I stop by and you can't even look me in the eye!"

"Nothing's different."

"Now that's a gosh darn lie."

Imani bit her lower lip. She didn't know how to tell Ajax about what she'd found. She didn't know how on earth she could confront him about something so unspeakable. The KKK was something out of mythology, not a real barrier to their relationship. It couldn't be.

"I don't really want to talk about it, okay Ajax? Maybe I just realized that we need some more barriers between us. I already told you, I'm not looking for a relationship."

"Right."

Ajax paused for a moment.

"Listen. If you don't tell me what's wrong, it's just gonna bother me. And I'm gonna want to come up here every day to find out why you can't look me in the eye. If you tell me now, you got a better shot of me leaving you alone."

Ajax looked into Imani's eyes and she saw that she was powerless to resist him. He had a point. Eventually, she'd give in. Eventually, the secret she'd discovered would be too much for her to ignore and it would come flying out of her mouth unfettered.

"When I was in the ranch house yesterday... I saw something," Imani said.

"In the old guest room?" Ajax asked.

Imani nodded.

"What did you find?" Ajax didn't seem surprised, but he also didn't seem like he had something to hide.

Imani had the suspicion that the robes she found weren't his. They couldn't be. No way he'd be reacting so... calmly.

"I know it was wrong but I couldn't resist the urge to... research... I opened up the big wardrobe and I found... robes... you know... white robes."

Ajax's face went white, but he didn't seem surprised.

"Sonuvabitch," He growled.

He wasn't surprised. Just upset. So he must have had some idea about his father's dealings, but perhaps he hadn't known the extent of them.

"Lester. They're Lester's."

"I figured," Imani said. Confirmation that the robes belonged to Ajax's father did shockingly little to assuage her fears that deep down, Ajax held the same dangerous, white nationalist beliefs. He was attractive as hell and he seemed to have a good heart, but that didn't mean that he was exempt from having a sinister side.

"But you still ain't eased up, huh..."

"Ajax, how am I supposed to believe that you aren't like him?"

"'Cause I ain't."

The answer was wholly unsatisfactory to Imani. Ajax seemed to find her discovery mildly annoying; he didn't seem to "get" the pain associated with it. It wasn't like finding out they had different tastes in music.

She was facing the fear that at his very core, Ajax wouldn't be able to understand her humanity. Imani wanted to believe in him, she just needed a little extra reassurance. She wanted to be sure about him.

"I can't just believe that Ajax. I'm sorry... Maybe you should just leave..."

"Leave?!" Ajax sounded like he didn't want to, but he stood up anyways.

"Yes. Leave. I... I don't need to be wondering if the guy I'm sleeping with is racist. I've been down that road before and it doesn't end well for me."

"Well I ain't no damned racist."

Imani walked towards the door and held it open.

"I'm sorry Ajax."

He started to walk towards the door and instead of leaving, he stood a foot away from Imani. She could feel his breath as he stood before her. She could smell his cologne. She could even feel the heat emanating from his flesh. She willed herself to say a final goodbye to get Ajax out of her hair.

"You don't want me to leave at all, do you?"

She looked up at him, trying to quell her nervousness now that Ajax had read her mind. Of course she didn't want him to leave. Of course she wanted him to fight, to prove that she was wrong, to confess that he hated his daddy and he'd do anything to keep her.

Whether or not she wanted Ajax was another story, but it would have been nice to feel wanted. Imani thought she must have been crazy. She barely knew Ajax yet she felt so much for him. She wanted him to want her badly.

Ajax smirked at Imani's silence.

"You really don't want me to leave... I bet I could get you into that bed right now if I wanted to."

Every logical part of Imani's brain was begging her not to give in to him. His lips touched her neck. Imani closed her eyes and still said nothing.

"I ain't my daddy Imani," He whispered into her ears.

He was too close for her to say no to him. Ajax began to nibble her earlobes and he repeated into her ear again, "I ain't my daddy."

Ajax was right. He could get her into bed if he wanted to. Imani tried to push herself to resist him.

She stuck her palm out and rested it against his chest, pushing away at him gently. That only steeled Ajax's resolve to pursue her. He wrapped his arm around her waist and pulled Imani away from the door. It slammed shut, closing them off to the world.

No one would have to know that her willpower had been destroyed. Franco wasn't here. No one was here. She could have Ajax one last time, and no one would know that she had put her dignity on the line for some hot, hot sex.

"Take me..." Imani whispered into his ears.

Exactly what Ajax wanted to hear. He picked Imani up off the ground and threw her onto the bed. He flipped Imani over onto her stomach and pulled the zipper on her pencil skirt down. Was he really going to do this? Did he want her so badly that he'd take her from behind. Imani enjoyed his rough hunger for her. Ajax said nothing and slipped Imani's pencil skirt off her hips. He didn't bother removing her blouse. She wore black cotton panties under her skirt and he pulled those off with ease too.

Ajax's hands ran over Imani's smooth umber colored ass cheeks. Her skin was soft and supple from he earlier shower and she smelled like fresh-scented lotion. Ajax spread her legs and climbed onto the bed between them. Instead of pulling out his hardness, he bent his head between Imani's thighs. She lay flat on her stomach and he thrust his head between her legs from behind.

Imani let out a loud moan as Ajax's tongue touched her pussy lips. He made her instantly wet and his tongue began to flick across her pussy lips, sending slow bursts of ticklish pleasure throughout Imani's body.

"Yes...." She gasped.

Ajax held her thighs still and drove his tongue deeper between her folds. Imani clutched the bedsheets and allowed his tongue's continued assault on her pussy. She thrust her ass backwards to meet his tongue while warm pleasure broiled between her thighs. Imani grew wetter and wetter as Ajax's thrusting tongue grew more ferocious and determined to bring her to climax.

Ajax's tongue even dipped dangerously close to Imani's asshole. She gasped as his tongue skipped past her most forbidden hole. He spread her ass cheeks apart and licked the full length of her pussy, allowing his tongue to linger on her asshole just a bit longer. Imani cried out as she climaxed and convulsed beneath Ajax's exploring tongue.

He couldn't resist her any longer. Watching Imani's thick, voluptuous bottom protruding upwards made him crave her wetness even more than usual. He stripped his pants off and hurriedly slipped protection onto his member. He spread her ass cheeks apart again and then drove his cock into her with one quick thrust.

Imani cried out again, a sound of surprise that sounded almost like bleating. She grabbed the bed sheets to brace herself as Ajax began to pound into her furiously. From this angle, his thick, long cock could still deliver a satisfactory amount of pleasure. In fact, Imani still seemed to grow wetter and wetter. Her juices collected in her pussy and her tightness grew hotter with each thrust.

"Yes... Yes..." She moaned. Another climax was close.

Ajax pummeled her furiously, watching her thick ass cheeks bounce with each thrust as he assaulted her pussy from behind. Imani spread her legs wider. Ajax used his thumb to massage her asshole as he drove his cock into her hard and deep. She groaned. And groaned again as two big climaxes took control of Imani's body. Ecstasy flowed through her in a seemingly endless stream.

Ajax stuck his thumb into her asshole just a bit deeper and she cried out as his large digit filled her ass and his cock rammed deeper into her pussy. He was close, she could feel it. Imani enjoyed the full sensation of being penetrated at both ends and she thrust her hips backwards to meet Ajax's thrusting.

"Cum for me... cum for me..." She whimpered.

Ajax grunted and thrust a few more times before releasing right into Imani's wetness.

He pulled out of her and then disposed of the condom. Their romp had been fast, but effective. Imani shuddered and then rolled over. She watched Ajax returning to the bed, unsure of what to do next. She'd tasted the forbidden fruit yet again. Imani wondered if there was really more to discuss here. Was she making a mountain out of a mole hill, or ignoring red flags yet again.

Ajax sighed as he got into bed with her. Imani turned to look at him and figured that she could postpone her worries, at least for a while. Imani didn't know how Ajax could get so much time off but she didn't bother asking him about it. She was just glad to see him again and to actually have him here.

"Ajax... Are your parents divorced?" Imani asked at some point after lunch.

Ajax turned towards her and wrinkled his nose.

"Why do you ask?"

"No reason, just curious."

"Listen Imani, you're great, but I don't wanna talk about my maw."

Imani understood difficult subjects. There were plenty of things that she didn't want to open up to Ajax about either.

"Alrighty. No need to talk about it. What about your dad, are you guys close?"

Ajax eyed her suspiciously before responding, "Are you investigating me?"

"No... I'm just trying to get to know you."

Ajax smirked.

"I see. Well, I can tell you that I ain't close to my paw. I work for him, I get paid, but that's about it. I'm just another employee on the ranch to him. I've always been like that from as early as I could lift a bucket of water."

"Wow."

Ajax continued, "I've worked on that ranch my whole life since before it was okay for me to be working 9-5. My paw ain't never said thanks, ain't never said he's loved me, even if I'm the only one he's got in this whole wide world."

"No siblings?"

Ajax smiled again.

"Not technically. Lester knocked up a twenty year old girl in town a few years ago. But she left with the baby so I've only met my little brother once."

Imani was getting a very grim picture of what

Ajax's family life was like. Ajax didn't seem to find it at all grim. He talked about everything that happened in Homer like it was just a matter of course. Imani tried her best to listen politely without revealing any of her horror or judgment. There were some things she couldn't help but judge, but she found the decency to hold her tongue.

"So what about dating," Imani asked, "Do you get out much in a town like this?"

Ajax chuckled, "Let's just say I have no trouble with the ladies. But it's hard to find someone I really connect with, you know?"

Imani bit down on her lower lip awkwardly. She knew Ajax was talking about her. While she shared his appreciation for their rare connection, she still felt uncomfortable acknowledging and talking about it. They were still relative strangers and while she liked so many things about Ajax, Imani was terrified of getting ahead of herself. She knew where that could lead and she wanted to hold off on developing feelings for someone knew.

It was like the moment she'd sworn off men, the most tempting guy she'd ever met crossed her path. As the late afternoon marched on, Imani and Ajax found themselves getting frisky again. Imani stopped worrying about getting too close to him or revealing too many of her cards at once. All of a sudden, the only thing that mattered was succumbing to Ajax's touch over and over again.

Her mind was closed to fear, closed to pain, and all she could do was whimper and moan as he brought her to climax over and over again until Homer was covered in darkness.

Testing

The next morning, Imani woke up early due to the buzzing from her cellphone. She shot a glance at Ajax, who was sleeping soundly, and she answered the phone in a whisper. Franco. Based on his hushed tones, he had figured out that Imani had a visitor. Her day of lovemaking had left her sore and tired. But at least her head didn't hurt anymore.

Franco informed Imani that they didn't have to work that morning, just wait for more tests to come from the lab back east in the afternoon. Apparently yesterday he'd sent the samples in a secure package overnight. Sometimes the government worked slowly, and other times it worked very quickly. Imani wondered if her trip out here would be cut short.

She hung up with Franco fast and noticed Ajax

rustling in the covers next to her. How had she gone from convincing herself she was through with him, back next to him. Imani was having second thoughts about her resistance to being with Ajax. She'd already given him a chance in so many ways, she was shockingly close to accepting his offer to take her out on a date.

Wouldn't that be a sight out here. An interracial couple in Homer, Oklahoma. Imani shuddered just thinking about the fact that would be an anomaly. Ajax's electric blue eyes snapped open and he groggily wrapped an arm around Imani. She allowed him to hug her and he wriggled his way upwards to kiss her on the cheek.

Imani closed her eyes, enjoying the sensation of his lips. Something about their clandestine encounters and Ajax's tender kisses made what was going on between them seem so forbidden.

"What's up with your funny friend?" Ajax said.

Funny? What did Ajax mean by that...

"You mean Franco?"

"Yeah..."

"I don't get it... What makes him funny."

It dawned on Imani that Ajax was referring to the fact that Franco was gay. She had no clue how he'd picked up on that. Franco wasn't exactly advertising his sexuality in Homer. He shared Imani's anxieties that the small town wouldn't exactly be the most accepting place.

"You mean you think he's gay?" Imani asked, trying not to betray Franco.

While she wanted to believe that Ajax was a safe person, she had no intentions of blindly trusting anyone in Homer, Oklahoma.

Ajax nodded.

"Sure."

"Listen, Ajax, whether or not Franco's gay... It doesn't matter okay? I don't know what things are like out here in Homer but it's just not a big deal in New York."

Ajax furrowed his brow, "So you think I'm some dumb homophobic hick?"

"No... That's not what I meant."

"Well it sure sounded that way to me," Ajax said curtly.

"You have to admit this town doesn't exactly seem... progressive."

Ajax scoffed, "Well I told you already, I ain't like anyone in this town."

Imani was bewildered. If he claimed to be so different from these townspeople, how could he live here? How could he call people family and friends who had klan robes draped in their closets like they were oft-worn three piece suits and not sickening white nationalist paraphernalia.

"If you aren't like the people here, how can you stay here?"

Ajax looked up at Imani like she'd made a point he'd never considered before. His expression transformed to a more mischievous one quickly.

"Well why don't we leave this town then. You and me..."

Imani could tell that Ajax was just crazy enough to be serious about what he was telling her. But she couldn't do that. She couldn't run away. She had a government subsidized lease in New York. She had a job. She had friends. As much as a whirlwind romance appealed to Imani in theory, in practice she was far too responsible to let her heart take the lead like that.

"I can't leave!"

"Well, I can. I'm here because I got a job, I can save up money and Homer is my home. But I ain't tied to these people Imani. I ain't gotta stay here. I know you think I'm just some backwards white trash guy but, that ain't who I am."

Imani bit down on her lip. She'd never thought of Ajax as white trash, but she could see how he'd misunderstood her. Imani had been judgmental. But she'd judged Homer, not Ajax. Now, she was seeing how that may have been perceived as the same thing. Imani knew it would be tempting to just run away with this cowboy, but it was crazy. They'd barely known each other a week. While her feelings for him were strong, they weren't "let's run away together" strong.

"Why can't you?"

Imani shrugged. Her desire to remain in Homer was mostly because it would be irresponsible to flee from her life. But another part of it was that she still didn't trust Ajax completely. She liked him, but she wasn't ready to take that big of a risk on him. She needed more than a few nights of incredible passion to decide on forever. Imani wasn't a risk taker, even if at the other end of the risk stood the possibility of unending bliss.

"Because I have responsibilities Ajax!"

He kept smiling.

"Maybe I can help you shirk some of these responsibilities this morning..."

He planted his lips on Imani's neck. Temptation flowed through her veins again. Ajax's eyes boring into her, his lips lingering on her neck, his gentle touch, all fueled her inability to resist him. Imani allowed his hands to trace the contours of her body and then he slid her body downwards so she was lying on her back.

Imani's head touched the pillow and Ajax swiftly positioned himself on top of her. Imani closed her eyes as Ajax's hand found its way up her nightdress. He fondled her stomach and squeezed on the soft flesh surrounding Imani's hips. She moaned as she felt his hands wander towards her pussy flesh.

Every bit of Imani's flesh was supple to Ajax's touch. He could feel his cock growing more tumescent as she relinquished herself to his touch. Ajax let out a deep growl of lust and Imani felt herself getting wetter at this verbal sign that he craved her. Imani hiked up her night dress and Ajax began to eagerly slip her panties off her waist. Imani grabbed onto Ajax's neck and pulled him close.

She planted her lips on his and drove her tongue into his mouth furiously. Her lust for him mounted. While Ajax had determined he would make love to Imani right there, she had a different idea...

She pushed Ajax onto his back more aggressively than she'd ever handled him before. At first, a look of surprise crossed over his face but that look was rapidly replaced with a look of pleasure.

Imani stripped off Ajax's undershirt, exposing his rock hard abs and perfect musculature. He was so hot in a way that differed from every overly groomed city guy. He was rugged, rustic, and everything about him oozed raw masculinity. His muscles tensed as Imani worked her way down to his boxer briefs. The tight pair of underwear hugged Ajax's thick strong thighs and outline the curvature of his bulging hardness.

She took control of the fabric, sliding it clumsily off of Ajax and exposing his hard cock to the cool air of the motel room. If Imani knew Franco well enough, he was probably out for a run or a nature walk so he wouldn't hear a single thing from their morning romp. Good. Imani had no intentions of keeping quiet.

Imani positioned herself between Ajax legs first. She grabbed his thick rope-like cock in her hands and then began to pump up and down. Ajax gasped as Imani wrapped her lips around his cock. The heat of his member pulsed into her mouth as she took the full length deep down her throat with ease. Ajax held onto Imani's head and guided her mouth slowly up and down his thickness.

"Mmm," She moaned.

His flesh grew thicker in her mouth and she could feel Ajax's ardent desires pulsating upwards from his hips. Her tongue flicked around his head and she enjoyed the taste of his flesh and the feeling of his heat pulsing into her mouth. Imani began to bob her head up and down. She needed to feel him growing in her mouth. She needed to feel his desire for her pulsing into her body.

Imani began to apply greater suction to Ajax's cock as she sucked him off. He grunted and closed his eyes, allowing her to work his magic on his long member. Imani's mouth stretched wide to accommodate Ajax's size. Ajax grunted as she took him deeper and deeper. Imani thrust his dick so deep into her mouth that her nose was mashed into Ajax's thick tufts of pubic hair.

She pulled her mouth off his cock, still slick with her spit. She used the lubrication to pump Ajax's dick with her hands while moving her mouth down to Ajax's velvety balls. They were close to his body as his arousal mounted. Imani gently stroked his balls with her tongue while her hands pleasured his cock.

Imani's tongue flicked across Ajax's balls and just when she thought he was about to finish, she switched it up again. Her mouth sucked hard on his bulging head and her hands massaged his lubricated balls. Imani made her blowjob wetter and wetter as she began to suck on Ajax's member more passionately.

"Oh yeah... Take it girl..." He grunted.

Encouraged by his words, Imani deep throated his cock over and over again. She choked on his dick but continued to take him as deep as he could go.

Imani felt his cock stiffen and she knew that Ajax was about to spurt into her mouth. She pumped his dick more furiously, focusing her mouth on the head and then twisting her palms around the base.

Ajax grunted and then released a hot load of cum into Imani's mouth. She swallowed each drop without tasting it and held Ajax's dick in her mouth until he went limp.

When she removed it, Ajax looked at her like she'd just revealed a startling secret.

"That. Was. Incredible," He said.

His tanned skin had flushed bright red and Imani realized that she'd almost sucked the life out of him. It didn't take long for Ajax to bounce back. After five minutes of lying on his back, he tapped Imani on the shoulder. She'd returned to her side of the bed, aching for him to find the energy to make love to her.

"If you get on all fours... I'll show you the time of your life," He said.

Imani grinned. They had plenty of time till the afternoon. And she had to admit, all that time playing hanky-panky in the bedroom with Ajax was excellent stress relief. She didn't think about bills, anxieties, work, or her ex. In fact, with Ajax she thought of nothing at all.

It especially didn't take much thinking for Imani

to get on all fours just like Ajax had requested. She pulled off her underwear and got into her position, arching her back and letting her nightdress slide upwards. Her ass and pussy were now fully exposed for Ajax's taking.

"Yes... Beautiful..." He muttered.

She watched his cock slowly come to life and then she felt Ajax position himself behind her. He massaged her ass cheeks slowly, teasing her with his gentle touch. She knew that what was coming next would be far from gentle. Imani braced herself as she felt her ass cheeks being spread apart and then Ajax dipping his hardness between her legs.

"Ohhhh," She groaned.

He was taking her slowly, appreciating the soft wetness of her entrance as he entered her for the first time that morning. Imani gasped as his thickness wormed its way inside her. Once Ajax's cock was fully embedded in her pussy, Imani started to thrust backwards slowly.

Ajax allowed her to bounce backwards on his dick for a few moments. She tried to get his hardness deeper and deeper, but she lacked the control to experience the full depth of his cock.

"Hold still," He growled finally.

Yes. This was the dominant man she knew. Ajax took his cowboy strength and firmly started to pound into her. Imani gasped. Loudly. Ajax pummeled her pussy from behind, driving between her wet pussy lips over and over again. The repeated sensation pushed Imani to climax quickly.

She'd been ready for him from the moment she'd pushed him onto his back. She needed him to thrust into her deeper. She needed him to dominate her and to force her into a world of pleasure far away from the anxieties of daily life.

"Yes..." She groaned.

"You like that huh? You like feeling my big hard cock!"

"Yes! Yes! I like feeling your big hard cock!" Imani moaned back.

She didn't know what had come over her. All of a sudden, she felt nasty and naughty and empowered by her naughtiness. With Ajax there were no barriers to pleasure. There was just ecstasy and freedom.

"Beg for it baby... Tell me how bad you want it..." He grunted.

As Ajax thrust into her Imani replied, "I want it so bad... Take me... Take me with your big hard dick..."

Imani was thrust over the edge. She clung to the bedsheets as she squealed. A climax bigger than any she'd ever known overwhelmed her. She moaned and whimpered in pleasure as the climax wracked through her body. Imani shuddered as Ajax continued to pound into her deeper and deeper.

"Oh yeah... You're so tight girl.... Oh yeah..." He groaned.

Still shuddering from her climax, Imani clenched her pussy tightly around Ajax's cock. As her wetness milked his cock for his seed, she thrust backwards. His thickness plunged deeper and deeper. Imani gasped for air with increased desperation. She could feel another climax building up deep within her.

Ajax's strokes grew slower and more measured. As he took her from behind slow and deep, he grazed more parts of her wetness. Imani gasped, enjoying their closeness as his hands rubbed all over her mahogany colored buttocks.

She let out a loud whimper and Ajax grunted. He pulled his cock out of her and released three hot spurts of his baby juice onto her back. Imani shuddered. Her sopping pussy was throbbing with satisfaction. Without Ajax's dick inside her, she felt empty. It would take a lot to come down from this high. Ajax moved off the bed quickly and used a warm towel to wipe the spunk off Imani's back.

He pulled her off the bed and looked her straight in the eye with a smirk.

"You look like you could use a nice shower to get cleaned up," He suggested.

"Oh yeah? Are you saying I'm a dirty girl?" Imani teased.

Ajax chuckled.

"I'm saying you're a very dirty girl... And maybe I can use a nice hot shower to whip you into shape."

"Okay cowboy, I'll take your word for it," Imani teased.

Imani tiptoed upwards and kissed Ajax on the lips. She fluctuated between certainty and confusion when it came to him. In bed together, everything was easy. It was clear that their chemistry was phenomenal and once they got started kissing, nothing could stop them from going further. But outside of bed, where Imani had to face reality, all she could see were barriers to their togetherness.

What represented reality and what didn't? Imani still couldn't figure it out.

Later that afternoon they had to go to Lester's farm. Franco was probably already out; Imani didn't notice his car out front.

At first, Imani was reluctant to arrive with Ajax. But he had offered her a ride and promised that everything would be okay. He promised that his father wouldn't care if they showed up together.

Based on what she had seen, Imani doubted that

was the truth. Plus, she cared. Imani still intended to be as professional as possible. She was still uncomfortable with how blasé Ajax seem to be about the entire fiasco with the Klan robes.

Could this really be that normal to him? How many other people in this town had a secret life where they fantasized about exterminating black folks.

Could she really handle a man who found KKK robes normal? Imani thrust the thought out of her mind as she readied herself to leave the motel.

She hopped into Ajax's truck, forcing herself to feel confident while doing so. As they drove down the flat empty roads towards the ranch her mind was racing.

She thought about that morning. She thought about how badly she wanted him. She thought about all the ways he helped her forget all the anxieties in her life. There was so much good about Ajax but the questions that brewed at the back of her mind planted seeds of doubt that had strong roots.

The rows and rows of corn were unlike anything in New York. The concrete jungle was fast-paced. You could smell cigarettes, coffee, donuts, and dust. Out here you can only smell when you're and that was it. The air was fresh and pure. Still, the emptiness not at Amani's mind. She wasn't used to it. Her world was one of fast cars, fast subways and fast food. Oklahoma was nice, but it wasn't home. And it could never be home, no matter how badly she liked Ajax.

As their car pulled up slowly to the ranch, Imani saw Franco's car waiting right there. Thank goodness. She didn't want to be stuck alone with Lester, and his son. It didn't matter how much she liked Ajax, some things were just awkward.

At least with Franco there would be a buffer and Imani would be less likely to experience something devastating.

But as the ranch came into view, Imani began to notice that something was awry. And that something had nothing to do with Ajax or her feelings for him.

She began notice to the white walls vandalized with red as if someone had pricked open the heart of the ranch house and allowed it's bloodied core to leak into view.

Her heart pulsated blood as red as the paint furiously through Imani's veins.

Ajax pulled his car to the front driveway, skidding across the earth. The paint grew clearer and Imani could make out the large red letters.

Her heart stopped and her mind started swimming as she read the words over and over, trying to convince herself that she was about to wake up from a twisted nightmare.

She had no clue who could have done this, but it was clear what their message was and it was clear what they wanted from her.

NIGGERS AND FAGS MUST DIE.

SOME RED PAINT dripped down from the letters like some sort of harbinger of doom.

The paint's uncanny resemblance to blood warned her what would happen if she stayed in Homer. And she wasn't alone. The hatred had been directed at Franco too.

Imani got out of the car and saw Franco leaning against their car. His face looked even more pale than usual. Instead of his usual effervescent smile, Franco looked stoic, stern and ultimately, scared.

Ignoring Ajax, Imani ran to her friend.

"Franco..." She began.

Franco nodded, a stark interruption and a plea for her not to speak the truth into reality.

Terror had ripped through both of their hearts.

They came from a place back east where hatred was at least kept under wraps.

Now, they were out in wild country. They were in the middle of nowhere where anything seemed to go as long as you proclaimed your love of the Lord, the Bible and guns.

Imani looked at Franco, asking him silently if they should approach the front door. She cast a glance backwards at Ajax. He seemed perturbed, but it wasn't the same thing that she felt or the same thing that Franco felt.

Being disgusted with an act of violence is very different from being the target of it. Now, Imani felt like she was more of a target than ever. Whatever Homer Oklahoma was keeping secret wanted to remain buried.

With a target on her back, Imani wasn't sure she was committed to finding out. She was an injured deer in a town of skilled hunters.

Franco possessed far more bravery than she did. He held her hand and they approached the door to Lester's Ranch. By then, Imani had stopped caring about Ajax and how he was responding to the big red letters against the stark white siding. Fear had taken over Imani and now instead of her new flame, she wanted her oldest friend by her side. They knocked on the door and waited for Lester's response.

The jitters sat high in Imani's chest. Her throat, her upper body and her heart all seem to vibrate at the same anxious frequency. She squeezed Franco's hand tightly. They heard Lester beginning to shuffle around the house, making his way towards the door.

Did he know about the paint that stained his white walls? Did he know who put it there?

Was it possible that even if Lester hated the vandal's destruction of his property, he somehow agreed with the violent words?

Imani found her hands sweating. She felt her heart racing and her head seemed unable to focus on anything but keeping her 2 feet planted to the ground. No one could ever predict how they would respond to racial violence and Imani was no different. When she heard Lester's footsteps getting heavier as he got closer to the door, she swallowed a huge gulp.

Franco could detect her fear. By the time Lester opened the door, they had dropped each other's hands and they put forth an appearance of confidence.

Imani could fake it well enough with Franco as an ally.

Lester seemed surprised to see them. That told

Imani he was at least aware of what had happened on the Redford Ranch.

Imani wondered if Lester had figured they would be scared away by the huge red letters. They bespoke danger, danger that any sane person would run away from.

Alone, she might have been afraid. But with Franco by her side, Imani felt a little more comforted and a little more secure in her ability to face this.

Lester opened the door with one of his customary grunts. Imani felt her heart racing but Franco cast a glance at her that let her know he would handle it and everything would be okay. Imani was more than happy to let Franco take the lead.

He opened the door slow.

"Y'all still around here?" He asked.

Franco replied with a smile that Imani knew she wouldn't have been able to muster.

Franco said, "Yes, we are still here. We noticed that you had some vandals."

Lester grunted and then replied, "Some of these new good kids. No doubt. Or maybe...

He seemed to be lost in thought.

Franco and Imani cast a glance at each other as if they weren't sure whether or not they should try to interrupt his train of thought.

Before they could decide, Lester spoke again.

"Or... It might've been some people angry 'bout all your investigating around here. Now don't look at me, I'm the one with all this rained soil you say. But I think I know who might not want y'all 'round the ranch. And I think I know who has it out for me and who wouldn't mind destroying my soil."

Franco and Imani weren't sure whether or not they should listen to Lester. They knew that he had it within him to lie, but they weren't sure he would destroy his own property. That didn't make much sense.

At the very least, they knew Lester was a business man. He cared about his money and he wouldn't do anything to jeopardize that. Now the factory upstream... That was a good candidate for suspicion. But a suspect left Imani with more questions than answers.

Lester came outside and he stood with them as they surveyed the white walls. Franco began to speak with Lester about how they could work on helping him remove it. It was almost like Franco was taking responsibility, like he felt guilty someone hated them and wanted them dead.

That was a reaction that Imani didn't agree with. But she knew that he was always the diplomat. It was just in Franco's nature to try to fix things.

As Franco discussed the logistics with Lester, she felt Ajax creeping closer to her. She felt him slip his hand in hers, a gesture that was likely intended to comfort her. Imani didn't know if she felt comforted. She didn't know if she needed comfort either. What she needed was to feel safe and she had a feeling she wouldn't get this profound sense of safety anywhere near Homer, Oklahoma

She could hear Lester's grunts as Franco spoke to him. She could hear them discussing hiring some kids in town to help remove the paint that was splattered all over Lester's wall.

But Imani had a sinking sense that removing the paint wouldn't stop whoever wanted them gone. They had been unwelcome here from the moment they set foot in town whether or not they've been environmental investigators or tourists just passing through.

Homer, Oklahoma stood in stark contrast to their identities and who they were as people. The best thing Imani had found here was Ajax.

But now, she had to wonder, was Ajax worth all of this? He was a great guy, but not even the best guy could make up for feeling scared all the time. For feeling like a walking target in a sundown town.

Plus, no matter how she felt for Ajax, that wasn't why Imani was out here. She was here to work, to enjoy the beauty, and then get out of town and go right back to New York. At least there she could walk down the streets at night without feeling afraid.

If that was what she wanted but not what Ajax wanted, they would be doomed. Perhaps, they had already been doomed from the very start. Imani resented the notion that they might be doomed. She was just beginning to admit to herself how she felt for Ajax. She could feel her affection for Ajax mounting in her chest. Her love of him was growing.

Imani hated to think that she really did love Ajax, but it was the only word she could think of to describe how he made her feel. It was different from how she felt with Brian. With Brian, love meant confusion and her heart raced for all the wrong reasons. And now, looking back Imani realized that Brian had no clue what love was and at the time neither did she.

She thought love was marked by tension, drama, and the constant yo-yoing of her emotions. None of these things represented what she felt with Ajax. There was never any uncertainty about how he felt for her.

She had been taught to think that uncertainty was good in the past. It meant there was still excitement. Imani was beginning to realize that security trumped excitement every day.

Having feelings for someone didn't always have to feel so terrifying. She didn't always have to feel like Ajax would be ripped away from her at a moment's notice. It was different. But everything with Ajax was different in a good way. If only she could reconcile the fact that he lived in a place like Homer.

Maybe if he lived somewhere else, somewhere more modern, she would be able to acknowledge out loud how he made her feel. Ajax warmed her to her very core.

"You alright?" He whispered into her ear.

Imani shook her head. No, she wasn't alright. And she couldn't pretend that she was this time. She was frightened. Imani wasn't yet willing to cut and run out of Oklahoma but she was close. Her drive to get to the bottom of this scientific mystery was the only thing keeping her here.

And of course, Ajax.

The graffiti that they found cut their visit short. Neither Franco nor Imani was interested in pursuing the business they'd originally intended to on Redford Ranch. Imani had to break away from Ajax, as she and Franco decided to return to their motel.

The truth was, she was still anxious about showing any public affection to him.

She and Ajax had been obvious enough whispering in the corner like teenage lovers. For now, Imani wanted her life to go back to being subtle and understated. Word got around this town whether she liked it or not. The red letters made it clear: she was an outsider and unwelcome.

Imani got into the car, sitting in the passenger seat next to Franco and both of them looked at each other as if they had much to discuss. Imani wasn't sure what he made of their entire visit. She had opinions of her own on Lester, on Ajax, and of course the hateful messages that had greeted them on the white walls of the ranch-house.

"You buy his story?" Franco asked as they pulled out of the Redford Ranch driveway.

As Imani threw one last wave in Ajax's direction, she had to stop and think. Did she buy his story? She had a hard time believing that Lester would destroy his own property. But at the same time, she also had a hard time believing that there is still sundown towns in the United States.

She was terrified for her life and for Franco's. That took precedence over deciding whether or not Lester was lying to her. She decided to share that sentiment with Ajax.

Ajax shrugged after Imani explained her fearful perspective.

"I'm scared. But what are they going to do? Don't think anyone around here is going to kill us."

Imani wasn't so sure. She knew that if they did die out here, no one would care about a mysterious, nameless, faceless pair of outsiders. Their deaths might be covered up by local police department. It had happened before in other parts of the country.

Imani was starting to feel very cynical about anything that might happen next in Homer Oklahoma.

"Well... If he's lying... Why would he vandalize his own property?" She said, trying to give Franco the benefit of the doubt and get her mind off of these morbid thoughts.

"Good question. People do funny things when they're trying to hide something."

That give Imani pause. If Lester was trying to hide something, did Ajax know about it? Had the answer to what they were looking for out here been underneath her very nose this entire time?

Still, Imani was hesitant to believe that Ajax was involved in anything sinister. If she had to believe that, she would have to believe that she had fallen for another man who wasn't worth a damn.

Another Brian, just dressed differently.

Klan Country

As nighttime fell on Homer Oklahoma, Imani began to feel more and more frightened. The words that had been plastered across Lester's house haunted her like a bloodied ghost. She was terrified, and more than terrified, she was afraid that this would drive a wedge between her and Ajax.

Their romance had been blooming and she was beginning to feel optimistic. That is, until she saw those red letters reminding her that she was an outsider. Homer could never be her home. The town rejected her fervently.

Dinner passed somberly. Franco tried his best to cook up a delightful meal but all Imani could think about was whether or not the doors were locked. Franco didn't seem to think that anything would happen to them that night, but Imani wasn't so certain.

She had given up on optimism when it came to Homer, Oklahoma and realized the sinister under belly fueling the town . But she ate. Franco had brought his Italian cooking out west to Homer and Imani tried her best to enjoy every bit of it.

Once they were finished with dinner, neither of them was in the mood to chat. They wanted no more talk of slurs or of anything that had happened earlier at Redford Ranch. They had talked enough for the day. Tonight was about decompressing and preparing for the challenges they would face the next day. Imani was certain these challenges would be far greater than either of them could predict.

As Imani settled into bed, she anxiously checked the locks on her doors two or three times. She began to change into something more comfortable when she heard a voice calling her from outside.

Ajax.

Apparently, what happened earlier had not scared him away. He was still pounding on her door, begging to be let in. For now, Imani was willing to have him. Although everything and everyone in Homer was on trial.

She opened the door and faced Ajax. The terror was quite visible on Imani's face. While he couldn't understand it completely, he tried his best to empathize with the woman he cared so much about. Ajax had stopped by the spend the night and hopefully keep Imani's mind off the threats against her life.

Imani opened the door and allowed Ajax to walk into her hotel room. She felt more nervous about everything. Nothing could change that, not even a visit from a man she cared about. What she'd experienced earlier was nothing small.

Imani could see Ajax's caring in his eyes. Unfortunately, it did very little to assuage her fears.

"How are you holding up?"

Imani appreciated him asking but she wasn't sure that there were any words to describe how she felt. She wasn't sure it was even something that Ajax could understand. There was no slur that packed the same punch as the n-word. There was nothing with the same painful history as far as Imani was concerned.

She tried her best to convey her feelings to him.

"I'm worried," Imani started, "I knew that things were a little bit different out here, but this is a whole new level. I'm worried about me. I'm worried about Franco. I'm worried that we won't be able to finish our work."

Ajax looked at her with understanding in his

eyes. Imani couldn't tell if he really understood her or if he was just faking it. Either way, she at least appreciated that he was trying. He had come here and he was trying to stand up for her and protect her like the man she needed him to be. It was surprising how many men chickened out when things got real. Ajax was no softie.

"I promise you Imani, I won't let anything happen to you. I'm here ain't I?"

Imani wished that could be enough. Knowing what she knew about Ajax's father, she wasn't sure that she could rely on him to pick her side over the other side if it really came down to that. There was a lot she wanted from Ajax, but she wasn't sure how much he was willing to give. Her fears that Ajax would be another man like Brian mounted along with the stakes between them.

"Are you sure? Would you really choose to protect me over..."

Imani trailed off. She knew that speaking the words out loud would bring a certain truth to light. The truth that Ajax's father was not a good person. Whether or not he had vandalized his property, he was still racist. And that was something that Imani had a hard time letting go of.

"You mean over my father? Don't you?" Ajax asked.

Imani nodded. She slowly raised her gaze to Ajax's. His blue eyes were locked onto hers and he was looking at her as if he wanted to sweep her up into his arms immediately. Imani wasn't quite ready for that yet. She needed to be sure about him. She needed to be sure that she wasn't just walking into another trap.

She needed to be sure that above all, Ajax was going to put her first. She needed to know that he would put her above Homer, Oklahoma and above his racist daddy. She needed to know that she was important to Ajax, important enough to risk losing everything.

Otherwise, what was the point? She was facing threats on her life out here in Oklahoma and she needed to know that Ajax would stand beside her.

"Of course I'll stand by your side over Lester Redford. He's given me a lot in life but he ain't been the daddy he thinks he's been. I promise you Imani, you come first with me. I hope you can believe me," He said.

He held his voice and his gaze steady. Imani admired his strength and his certainty.

Imani looked into his eyes and saw that they were honest. He genuinely cared for her and at least he believed that he would stand up for her in favor of his father. Whatever past Ajax had with his father had apparently been quite difficult.

As Imani looked into Ajax's eyes, she wanted him to wrap her in his arms and hold her close. She wanted Ajax to use his kisses to baptize her clean and wash away the pain that she'd experienced out there on the ranch. She wanted Ajax's love to cleanse her, to make her forget her troubles just like it always did.

"Kiss me," she begged, or maybe demanded.

Either way, Ajax complied. He pressed his hot lips to hers and she closed her eyes savoring the flavor of his tongue. His lips moved from hers to her cheek, to her chin, to her neck. Imani just stood there allowing him to kiss her, experiencing each divine kiss as a moment in time she would never be able to get back.

Although fleeting, these precious moments were revving her up and driving her towards wanting more. Ajax could always bring the wild thing out of her even when her heart was gripped by a devastating terror.

Ajax's hands began to wander down Imani's hips and he gripped her bum, pulling her close to him. With her arms wrapped around him she kissed him back. The ferocity of their kisses pulled them further and further away from the stress of the day.

Imani inhaled deeply as Ajax squeezed her

buttocks. She loved feeling small and protected in his arms. He pulled her closer and then lifted her off the ground. Imani wrapped her legs around Ajax's strong torso and wrapped her arms around his neck. He allowed her hands to run through his longish blond hair. His lips remained pressed to hers. And his tongue probed furiously down her throat.

Ajax's smell infiltrated Imani's nostrils slowly. With each breath, with each pulsating beat of her heart, she felt her hunger for Ajax growing deeper and deeper. She was ready to put the day behind her now. Knowing that Ajax would protect her was almost more meaningful than knowing he loved her.

Imani wondered if he did. He was here, trying to protect her, trying to be with her. He was kissing her like he loved her. They made love like two long-lost lovers. Everything that existed between them was reminiscent of love. But a nagging feeling in Imani's chest told her to wait before speaking those three powerful words that could bind her to Ajax in a way she wasn't sure she was ready for.

She continued to kiss him and to Hunger for him as his hands continued to wander over the softest and fleshiest parts of her body. They both wanted to go faster but Ajax kept the pace slow and steady.

Ajax walked over to the bed and lay her down on her back. Imani closed her eyes as he positioned himself on top of her. Now his hands didn't just clutch at her hips, they roamed over her body and Ajax groped at Imani's soft plump breasts. She gasped as he began to strip her down to nothing and as his hands squeezed at her nipples.

"Ohh..." Imani moaned.

She was ready and waiting to forget everything that had happened that day. All she needed was Ajax to urgently thrust his prick into her. She reached forward, pawing at his cock and begging for him to just put it inside her and dull the pain of waiting. Ajax ogled Imani's naked body as he continued to touch her and kiss her. He could tell that she wanted him urgently but he wanted to take his time with her and experience every bit of Imani's flesh.

Ajax's fingers began to slide between Imani's pussy lips as he kissed her. She arched her back, allowing him greater access to her wetness. She was slick with anticipation. Feeling Ajax's fingers slide into her warmth was one of the best feelings in the world, especially after a long day like this one. Ajax started sliding in two fingers at once into Imani's pussy. She cried out and her pussy clenched tightly around Ajax's fingers. He began to squeeze his fingers in and out of her wetness. Imani gasped as Ajax fingered her slowly, grazing her g-spot with each thrust of his fingers.

She gasped with each stroke, desperate for him to replace his fingers with his thick cock. Ajax continued to plunge his fingers into Imani's wetness until she was gasping madly for breath, lingering on the verge of climax.

"Yes... Yes..." She cooed.

Ajax began to finger Imani's wetness more furiously. She clutched his tense muscular back as his hard fingers pushed deeper and deeper. Suddenly, her mind accessed the pleasure it had been searching for. Imani's hips bucked upwards aggressively as she came. Imani started to moan and quiver beneath Ajax's hands.

With two fingers inside her, he used his thumb to begin rubbing Imani's clit. Imani continued to moan loader and louder. The waves of her orgasm continued throbbing within her pussy as Ajax pressed his finger gently to her hardened nub.

"Yes! Yes!" Imani cried out.

Ajax appreciated her encouragement. Imani stared into his eyes as he continued to finger her. As he watched her face twisted up in pleasure, Ajax felt his chest swelling up with what he assumed was love. Ajax had been with plenty of women in Homer, Oklahoma, so it wasn't that he was inexperienced that way.

But when it came to love, Ajax was definitely

inexperienced. He had never felt for another woman what he felt for Imani. He had never looked down at a woman's face and thought she was the most beautiful woman in the world. He had never wanted to protect someone the way he wanted to protect Imani. As Ajax thought about his love for her, his desire to make love to her mounted.

His cock slowly grew tumescent and he undressed quickly. Seeing Ajax's dick spring into view, Imani began to grow even more excited. She reached her palm out to grab onto his cock but Ajax pulled away.

"Patience, darling," He said with his typical devilish smirk.

Imani's chest heaved impatiently and she pouted. She'd waited long enough for Ajax to slip between her legs, she wasn't looking for another game.

"Don't get all mad princess. What's comin' is comin'. Get on all fours..."

Imani cheered up once she heard Ajax's command. She wanted it hard, rough and fast and apparently Ajax wanted the same thing. Imani positioned herself on all fours and arched her back. Her smooth skin glimmered in the evening light. Imani's mind had wandered far away from the stress earlier that day.

Ajax slipped on a rubber and then positioned himself behind Imani in bed. He lovingly stroked her ass cheeks, enjoying the sensation of her soft skin beneath his palms. He looked at her pussy, bulging with arousal and desire for entry, and felt his cock jump. Ajax needed her now, he'd already waited long enough for her.

Ajax began to slide his dick into her slowly. Imani felt tighter than usual; just getting Ajax's massive dick head past her entrance felt like a tight squeeze. She grit her teeth as he slid in the head and then started to slide in the rest of his dick.

"Ohhh!" Imani gasped as she tried to accommodate his size.

"Easy girl..." Ajax cooed.

Imani relaxed her muscles and arched her back to give him better access to her wetness. Ajax slipped the rest of his cock inside her and the pain subsided. All Imani could feel was pleasure. She gasped loudly as Ajax began to move his dick in and out of her wetness. Each stroke was slow and measured. His cock grazed every inch of her tightness as he moved. Every cell in both of their pleasure centers was alight with erotic hunger. Ajax's motion stimulated Imani's desire and vice versa.

They fed each other's hunger for each other and began to propel each other closer and closer to climax. Ajax took his work-hardened palms and spread apart Imani's ass cheeks as he pounded her from the back. He caught sight of her tiny puckered asshole and craved taking her there too.

Imani threw her hips back and swiveled her butt onto his dick in controlled motions. His dick stiffened as she took control of their love making. As he watched Imani's perfect mahogany ass swiveling around his pale pink cock, he couldn't help but feel a climax approaching furiously.

"Slower... slower..." He breathed.

Imani drew in a slow breath as she too approached a climax. She succumbed to Ajax's desires for her to take it slow. She swiveled her hips like an erotic belly dancer, undulating her ass cheeks and allowing her pussy to swallow Ajax's cock at a sedated pace.

"Yes..." He grunted.

Imani knew they were both on the verge of being edged over into climax. But she didn't pick up the pace or turn their slow love making into an urgent race to the finish. She continued to swivel her hips and allow her pussy to engulf Ajax's hardness.

"I'm cumming... I'm cumming..." Imani whimpered as a climax finally started in her core and emanated out to every inch of her body.

Imani began to quiver and tremble, throwing

control back into Ajax's hands. His cock continued to pierce her pussy a little faster now as she rutted and groaned in climax. With a few more hard, deep thrusts, Ajax felt his balls tighten close to his body. Cum erupted from the tip of his cock in thick spurts as he orgasmed. Ajax shuddered and gasped loud for breath. His hands were gripping Imani's ass cheeks tightly as he finished.

They had both been eager for satisfaction and their climaxes had been deep, slow and beyond satisfying. Ajax slowly pulled his cock out of Imani's wetness and they cleaned up, crawling into bed together. As Imani lay next to Ajax, she imagined whispering the words "I love you" to him right there. Her desire to stay in control of the situation with Ajax was the only thing that prevented her from spilling her feelings to him.

Ajax's hard body pressed up against hers as they lay together naked. Their hands drifted towards each other and their fingers interlocked, a wordless way of speaking their commitment to each other. Their emotions danced between the spots of flesh where their bodies were pressed together. But still, neither of them said a single word. Imani was prepared to break the silence by initiating a second round of lovemaking when she heard a few noises that she couldn't place.

"Do you hear that?" She whispered.

Ajax scrunched his face up, "No... What are you hearing?"

"Sh... Listen..." Imani hissed.

The room fell silent and the two of them listened. At first, Imani thought she was going crazy and imagining phantom sounds. The red paint on the ranch house had impacted her more than she realized perhaps.

But then, Ajax heard it too.

"I hear something," He said, leaping out of bed and jumping into his boxers immediately.

Imani sat up in bed, her concern covering every inch of her face. Ajax indicated that he wanted her to stay still.

The sounds from outside grew louder and Imani had a feeling that she wasn't just being paranoid. Ajax threw on a plain white T-shirt and she watched as he approached the window. His arm was still stuck out, with his palm turned towards her telling her that he wanted her to stay very very still.

Imani's heart was racing. Ajax pulled the curtain back ever so slightly and peered outside.

Imani knew what he wanted from her, but she also knew that she couldn't stay still not knowing what he saw outside. Her curiosity got the better of her reason.

She slipped into her nightdress and then wrapped a white bathrobe around her body cinching it tightly at the torso.

Against Ajax's wishes, Imani moved towards the window as well.

As Imani's eyes caught what was happening outdoors, the fear she felt in her chest was something she knew she would never be able to describe at a later date. If she ever got to see that later date. Outside the motel, men in white robes with tall pointed masks walked around in a circle. Except their walking was more like marching. And they marched in such a symphony that you could almost forget the pure evil behind the masks.

Some of them were carrying guns, others were holding large stakes alight with flames. The flames illuminated the dimly lit parking lot giving Imani full view of the well used white robes.

She morbidly wondered how many Klansmen had received their robes from their daddy or granddaddy.

Their chanting was growing louder and louder. Their boots hit the pavement in a terrifying order. The marching and the chanting were harbingers of the danger that Imani had predicted from the moment she saw the red paint splattered across the Redford Ranch.

She was too scared, beyond scared, yet she remained glued to the window as she watch the Klansmen chant and march in a circle around the parking lot of her motel.

They were here. They were coming for her. Imani knew that right now, more than ever before, her life was at risk. All she had standing between her and those men was Ajax and the flimsy motel door.

"Imani get away from the window," Ajax said sharply.

Imani could tell that he was trying to act like he was in control but really, he was just as scared as she was. The sight outside meant that Homer was no longer safe for him. It had never been safe for Imani, but she still hadn't expected this level of danger. And Ajax probably hadn't either. To him, Homer had probably been an idyllic town -- not this dark place of hatred.

Her first instinct was to get Franco, but first she had to listen to Ajax. She pulled away from the window and slipped to the door that separated her part of the suite from Franco's. She knocked, but heard nothing. Perhaps he was already fast asleep, or perhaps the TV was too loud, or perhaps he was listening to Prince records. Imani banged on his door again. Still nothing.

She began to make her way back towards Ajax

when he interrupted her with a sharp command, "I told you, stay back."

Imani knew he was scared. She had never heard Ajax speak to her like this and even if his voice was steady, the undertones of fear still seeped through to her auditory pathways. She remained still, frozen in place in the center of the room as the chants grew louder still.

There were probably over fifty men congregated in the parking lot. Imani imagined there were some women too. The snide looks from women in the town hadn't gone unnoticed.

They were silent for a while. Imani could tell that Ajax was trying to make out the words they were saying. But before either of them could hear anything too clearly a gunshot went off. The sharp burst of the bullet rang through the air and Imani let out a terrified shriek.

If their mission was to scare her, they'd been successful.

"Get behind the bed," Ajax said.

Imani didn't need to be told twice; she fled behind the bed and pressed her body tightly against the floor. She knew that no matter how well she hid, no matter how far away she stayed from the window, if the folks outside wanted to get her, they would.

The terrifying sound of their boots hitting the pavement and the hateful chanting coming from their mouths brought Imani close to the point of fainting. She had never felt such terror in her life. She had never been in such a fight to survive.

"Dang I really wish I had my gun," Ajax muttered.

From her position behind the bed, Imani couldn't figure out how on earth adding another gun into the mix would make things better.

Bang! Another gunshot. She flinched as she heard that one and curled up small in a ball behind the bed. Imani could feel herself shaking uncontrollably. The chanting and the marching continued and Ajax maintained his post by the window.

"They better not come up here," he said angrily.

Again, Imani wasn't exactly sure what he thought he could do. In a sense, the men who had come into the parking lot had already won. Imani was terrified out of her mind and she was just waiting and hoping they would go away and leave her in peace.

That was the only thing she could do: lie there and wait for it to be over. Here, she was powerless in a way she wasn't accustomed to being. Strength and independence didn't help while she feared for her life.

If Ajax weren't here, she would be going through this completely alone. Imani said nothing as she lay there. She couldn't bring herself to speak. But the silence terrified her even more as the loud boots against the pavement pounded in her head at the same harried rate of her heart.

Imani just wanted it all to stop.

After a few minutes, the sounds didn't die down. The chants turned into screams and hollers. The gunshots went off into the air one after the other. Imani could no longer flinch in time to keep up. All she could do was fly her hands over her ears and hope and pray that it would be over soon.

Franco emerged from the shared space. Apparently, some of the gunshots had woken him up and he moved towards the window where Ajax was standing in his matching pajama set.

Imani couldn't imagine how terrified Franco felt too. While he didn't share her skin color, Franco was just as hated by those men in their white robes with their tall pointy masks hiding their faces from view.

Franco stood with Ajax and the two of them seemed to be muttering under their breath what Imani could only assume was a plan. From her position on the floor, she was coming up with a plan too. Except this plan was much different from anything Franco or Ajax were coming up with.

Imani had a plan to get out of Homer the moment this died down. So long as she survived, she intended to leave. There was nothing left for her here. The boss would have to understand.

After 45 minutes of hooting, hollering and firing off their guns, the men finally marched off. Their scare was complete. Their threats had been laid out like clues but Imani wasn't really looking to solve this particular mystery.

She waited before getting up from her position on the ground until both Ajax and Franco crouched down next to her and soothed her over and over, promising that everything would be okay.

Except, it wasn't okay. Nothing about this was remotely close to being okay.

Eventually, Imani got up. She was still shaking in fear as both Franco and Ajax led her to the small kitchenette. Franco made all three of them a mug of tea and they sipped their chamomile brew somberly. Franco was still dog tired and he retired the moment he hit the bottom of his drink.

Imani was left with Ajax but she didn't share Franco's exhaustion. There was no way she could spend another night in Homer. Or at least, not another day.

Imani thought it through and while she couldn't escape in the middle of the night, she silently planned to be free of Oklahoma by the next morning.

She refused to talk about what had happened with Ajax. She claimed that all she needed to feel better was to crawl into bed with him.

They bolted the motel room door and checked it twice. Imani climbed into bed with Ajax, knowing in her heart and her head that this would be the last night they spent together. She would never come back here, she couldn't.

Imani's head filled her night with horrible dreams. Despite those dreams gnawing at her psyche she still slept well enough. The next morning, Imani woke up early energized by her plans to flee. Ajax was sleeping soundly, and she wondered if he had been tossing and turning alongside her. Imani knew she couldn't wonder about that for too long, she had work to do.

She pulled her suitcase out from the cupboard and quickly began thrusting her clothes and electronic devices into it as fast as possible. Now she would have to work out some ride to the airport. There were a couple cab drivers in town who hadn't seemed too opposed to carrying a black woman in their car. Someway, somehow she was going to leave here.

When she was mostly done packing, Ajax rose

from his sleep. He sat up in bed and watched her putting her things away for a few moments before he realized what was happening.

"What are you doing, Imani?" He asked.

Imani sighed and then told him, "I'm leaving Homer Ajax. I'm sorry... Things have been great for us... but I can't stay here anymore."

"So you're just going to get up and leave?" Ajax asserted.

Finding out that Imani was about to cut and run roused him from his sleep even faster. He was still wearing his white T-shirt and boxers from the day before. Imani looked at his perfect body with sadness. This wasn't how she intended to leave him but there was no easy way to do this. She just had to rip the Band-Aid off and run. Another night in Homer might cost her life.

Imani wasn't willing to pay that price.

"What choice do I have, Ajax?"

"You could stay. You could trust that I would protect you," he said.

Imani scoffed, "Did you see what happened last night? One man isn't going to stand between me and death. I'm no fool. I'm getting out of here."

Ajax looked on at her furiously. His eyes had turned icy blue and his face began to redden. She could tell that he had so much to say but she wasn't exactly ready to hear it.

"What? You think I should stay here and rest risk my life?"

"You could. There are reasons for you to stay in Homer," he said.

Imani felt a pang of guilt in her chest. But she had already made up her mind and there was no turning back.

"I'm sorry Ajax... But there is no reason for me to risk my life and stay out here. I can't."

"So I was foolish to think I meant anything to you?"

Imani bit down on her lower lip. If she acknowledged that she loved Ajax now, that would only complicate things and make leaving more difficult than it needed to be.

"Well fine. You were just a good lay anyways," he muttered bitterly.

Imani watched him with her mouth agape as he threw on his pants and walked out of their motel room without another word.

She had ripped off the Band-Aid but it hurt far more than she had ever expected.

Return Ticket

∽

With Ajax gone, Imani set about getting herself to the airport. She found a cab number and she began writing a note to Franco. Above anyone else, Franco would understand what could possibly propel her to disappear from Homer without a second word. Franco must have been out for a run because by the time Imani's cab arrived, she hadn't seen him at all that morning and he didn't stop her from taking her things and then getting into the cab.

Imani didn't say much to the cab driver as she got in. Today, she wasn't in the mood for making friends. He informed her that the drive to the airport would cost $250 and it would take three whole hours. Imani was sure there was a shorter way but she wasn't in the mood to haggle over pricing. As she sat in the car, she used her phone to book a flight back east.

"Doin' alright miss?" The cab driver asked a few minutes in.

"Yes," Imani replied shortly.

"Mind if I play country music?"

"No, I don't mind."

And in truth, she didn't. Imani couldn't think of a more perfect serenade as she high tailed it out of Oklahoma. As they were driving down the main roads, she could have sworn she saw Ajax. But it wasn't him — just a man who looked like him. As Imani thought about the fact that she was really leaving Ajax behind in Homer, she started to cry.

Grateful that she was sitting in the back seat, Imani leaned her head against the window and began to let the tears spill out. She hadn't allowed herself to feel anything since the past night, but it just start to hit her that she would never see Ajax again. His sweet smile, his blue eyes and his boisterous laugh would all be a thing of the past.

Imani knew she didn't deserve Ajax. He'd been nothing but sweet and charming and she'd dashed off as soon as things got difficult. She'd never smell his sweet scent again and she'd never see his face. Imani tried to picture their last kiss but she could hardly remember already. The night had been so hectic that the last time they'd made love had transformed into a blur and Imani could hardly pluck out any specific images.

She started to sob harder and harder, growing more tempted to beg the cab driver to turn things around. She could run back into Homer and grab Ajax by the hand, begging him to leave with her. Imani talked herself down from another impulsive decision. She'd already done enough by running off. The best thing she could do was just commit to leaving and never look back, never causing Ajax any more hurt.

The three hour ride to the airport wound long and slow. The country music blared in the background. Imani listened until she got sick of it, but she never asked the cabbie to change the station. When they pulled into the airport parking lot, Imani hesitated before checking in. As she walked up to the counter, she felt herself being pulled backwards. Was this regret?

Before Imani could reach the check-in line, Franco called.

"You've left, haven't you?"

Imani felt tears coming out of her eyes but she resisted the urge to cry.

"Yes. I've left," She said.

Franco detected the heaviness in her voice.

"Figured as much. So I went on without you this morning. We've discovered something about those soil samples I think you'll want to hear. But we're in FBI territory now so I'll be joining you in New York in a day or two."

"FBI territory?"

"Listen, I don't wanna talk about it over the phone. The walls have ears and all that. The boss says there's no chance he wants this information getting out."

"So what? I should still leave?"

"You bet your ass you should. After last night... I don't know Imani. Just stay safe. I'll see you in New York in a couple of days."

Imani hung up before Franco could ask her about Ajax. She knew he was probably thinking it — how could she leave behind the cowboy she'd spent all those weeks in bed with?

Imani sighed and made her way to the short check-in line. Yes, I'm flying to New York. No, I would not like an upgrade to first class. Well if I get the discount then, sure. Imani scribbled her name and address onto a pair of labels and fastened them to her small rolling suitcase and her handbag. This was it. She was leaving Oklahoma. Passport and ticket in hand, she began to make her way to security.

The line was longer here. Leaving Oklahoma was apparently more popular than coming in. Imani gripped her belongings and stood in line, thanking the Lord silently that soon she'd be in a place where her blackness wasn't an anomaly. Down to the last minute she was receiving stares that questioned whether or not she belonged.

As Imani neared the line, she heard her name.

Imani whipped her head around but saw no one. She heard her name again.

"Imani! Imani!"

She turned her head again and saw him. Ajax. He was running through the airport like a scene out of a movie, avoiding women with strollers and slow moving folks who had adopted a leisurely pace.

"You're next ma'am," The guard called.

But Ajax was here. Ajax. He must have been right on her tail the entire time. Imani couldn't go through security now. She stepped out of the line, underneath the barrier and Ajax ran up to her wrapping her in a huge hug.

"You're here. You're still here thank God. I thought I missed you."

Imani let herself get wrapped up in Ajax's arms and enveloped by his smell. She didn't say anything and neither did she. Secretly, she was relieved that he'd even come here in the first place. They hadn't exactly parted on good terms so Imani wondered what on earth had been so important that Ajax had left the ranch and traveled three hours just to chase her down.

"Ajax —," Imani started.

"Hush for a minute..." He said, holding her close again.

Imani felt her heart racing. She wanted him to just say those three little words; more than that, she could feel the words spilling out of her mouth too.

Ajax pulled away and Imani stared into his blue eyes, just waiting for him to say something.

"I couldn't just let you leave like that Imani... I... I... love you."

Imani's heart swelled as she heard Ajax finally confessing what she had been hoping he felt. The same emotions had been throbbing in her heart for weeks but her uncertainty about Ajax had prevented her from just saying "I love you". The tension surrounding the phrase and all its implications had built up for weeks but the moment Ajax confessed his affection, it just felt normal.

"I love you too, Ajax..."

"Don't you ever run off on me like that again," He chastised.

Imani looked up at him and nodded.

"I promise."

Ajax bent his head to hers and they kissed. Although in terms of time they hadn't been separated that long, there had been a gulf between them since the previous night. As they kissed Imani felt the wounds that had been festering between them begin to heal. Ajax's soft lips restored life to her.

Imani pulled away, "So you came here to tell me to stay?"

"Sort of... Imani... We need to talk... You can't leave Homer, not yet."

"What's going on?"

"I know some things about Lester and I ain't exactly been honest with you..."

"Can it wait?" Imani asked.

"Yeah... It can wait..."

"Let's get out of here then. I'll call Franco, you can tell me everything that's going on and we'll head back to Homer tomorrow."

"All tuckered out, are you?"

Imani nodded, "Plus, I don't want to be caught in Homer after dark."

They exchanged knowing glances about the events that had occurred the previous night. Ajax picked up Imani's bag and began to carry it towards the exit.

"Come on, I know a motel not too far from the airport we can stay tonight."

"And it's safe?" Imani asked.

Ajax nodded, "I promise you it's safe. Plus this time, I came armed."

Imani forgot all about the cost of the plane ticket and she forgot about returning to New York. New York could wait, but Ajax couldn't. Imani couldn't wait to get holed up in a hotel room with him for more reasons than one. Once they were in the front of the airport, they made their way to Ajax's pickup truck. He helped lift Imani into the passenger feet. Her shoes tapped against a huge chunk of metal.

Ajax hadn't been lying about coming armed. He threw her suitcases into the backseat, got into the driver's seat and started driving away. Imani's day had been such an emotional roller coaster. She was living a life that wasn't hers, characterized by one impulsive decision after another. If she hadn't known any better, she would have claimed that loving Ajax was making her crazy.

They pulled into the parking lot of a small but updated hotel. There were plenty of vacancies and Ajax paid for the largest room they could find. Sometimes Imani forgot that money was really no object to him. Whenever his father passed away, he was his sole heir. Plus he made a cool six figures from managing the ranch.

Ajax carried her bags upstairs himself and they

sat in the room quietly as Ajax put on a pot of coffee. Imani was just breathing deeply, trying to align herself with everything that had happened. First, she was done with Ajax. But then, he'd chased after her, driving a cool three hours out of town just to stop her flight.

She knew that a part of him had done it for love, but she also knew that couldn't possibly be the only reason. Ajax seemed nervous and he seemed like he was hiding something. Based on the call she'd received from Franco, Imani guessed it was something pretty big.

The coffee maker beeped and Ajax poured two styrofoam cups of steaming coffee. Or at least it was supposed to be coffee.

"I'm sorry to be all mysterious Imani... It's just... We're talking about my father here right. I know he ain't a good guy... I know that... But he's still my paw. He's still the man who took me to little league games, who got me this job, who sent me out to Texas for college..."

"I get it. When dealing with family, things get complicated."

"Lester's hiding something. My maw... She left when I was ten right... But I never heard from her since. Not a word. I've been writing to her, looking for her, but she's just disappeared."

. . .

"You think your dad has something to do with it?"

Ajax shrugged, "That I don't know. But I think he must've done something to scare her off at least. Scare her so bad she don't even want to be found by her own son."

Imani nodded empathetically, waiting for Ajax to continue.

"The guys who own the factory... My father's in bed with 'em. Not... Literally... But he's been getting money from 'em to look the other way when they dump waste into the river. But the guy... the main one... Chuck Lansbury, he pissed Lester off real bad. And now I think Lester's framing 'em for all the pollution on his ranch. I don't know what he's looking for... A lawsuit... Something."

Imani's heart was racing. That meant Lester could have very well vandalized the ranch himself. He could have called up his Klan buddies to terrify her and Franco. It made sense that he could be behind it all.

"But if Lester is doing this... I mean... It's illegal!"

Ajax nodded, "I know. It's why I didn't want to tell you. But I had to Imani. You understand, right?"

Imani wasn't sure if she understood why Ajax

had slept on this secret for so long and then decided it was worth bringing to light.

"I had to, because I care about you. I love you. And I needed to show you that no matter what happens or what happened in Homer, I'll always be on your side and your side alone."

Imani set her coffee down and straddled Ajax on the couch. She held his face, letting her hands graze against his growing dirty blond stubble. Then Imani kissed him. This was a long, slow kiss. She closed her eyes and took in the scent of Ajax's cologne, the sensation of his hard-worked skin beneath her palms and of course the feeling of his hardness rising in his pants.

Imani ground her hips into him as she kissed him. Her heart raced faster as her hunger for Ajax grew. She knew that calling Franco should have been her next step but she couldn't help want to take things slow. Franco would be there all night and she'd gone long enough without Ajax's touch.

"Kiss me," She whispered.

Ajax's hands gripped her thighs and he pulled her even closer as he kissed her. Imani could feel her pussy growing wetter and wetter the more Ajax kissed her. He stood up, gripping her butt cheeks tightly. Ajax leaned Imani against the wall and continued to kiss her lips and neck. With her back pressed hard against the wall, Ajax began to work her shirt over her head. Imani wasn't sure how he balanced her, but she never feared falling over as he took off her shirt and unhooked her bra. Her breasts swung into view and Ajax immediately bent his head to take her magnificent tit flesh into his mouth.

She moaned as his tongue lapped around her nipples and she held his head still, forcing him to continue pleasuring her breasts. Ajax moved his head to her other nipple and both dark circles had transformed into hardened nubs. Imani gasped and Ajax removed her from her position against the wall and slammed her into the bed hard.

Then he began to speed things up. Good. Imani had no desire to take it slow.

"I love you," She whispered.

Those words sent Ajax wild. He stripped off her pants and underwear, leaving Imani completely exposed in bed. Then, he stripped down to nothing. His muscular physique pulsated powerfully as he joined her in bed. As he climbed between Imani's legs, she grabbed his dick and positioned it at her entrance. Enough foreplay, she wanted hot, hard and fast action as soon as possible.

He began to slide into her slowly. Imani clutched his butt cheeks pulling him deeper. She gasped as Ajax's thick cock began to stretch her walls. Ajax stared deep into her eyes watching her face twist and contort as he thrust into her inch by inch.

Imani groaned loudly as he buried himself inside her up to the hilt. She whispered his name into his ears begging him to start thrusting, begging him to use her harder and faster.

Ajax steadied himself on the bed and began to thrust his cock into Imani's wetness

Ajax began to plunge into her ferociously. His hunger for her was visible on his face and she could feel how much he desired her flesh. He buried his thick ropey cock into her tight satiny heat as she gasped and gasped in pleasure.

The intermingling of her screams, gasps, and moans drove Ajax wild. He grunted as he pounded into her feverishly. The sensation of his thick cock pushing past her lips sent pleasure shooting through Imani's body.

She knew that she would climax soon. Ajax could see her desire on her face; he could see that she was edging closer to a beautiful release. His cock stiffened and he worked to quell an eruption of his own until after he was certain Imani had been satisfied.

Imani knew that this climax would transport her to another world. This was what happened when you were in love. Somehow, getting into bed with

Ajax felt more special, more important than any of the other times they had slept together.

Their confessions of love confirmed that what they had been feeling every time they made love was real. Somehow this urban black girl and this white country rancher had fallen in love.

They'd shared fears and secrets. They'd shared laughter. And of course, they'd shared in the pleasures of the flesh.

"Harder. Take me harder," Imani moaned breathily.

"Mine... This pussy is mine..." Ajax grunted.

Imani loved hearing him claim her like that. She was his. His pussy, his woman, his incredible lover.

Imani dug her nails into his ass cheeks trying to pull him even deeper. They were rutting like animals in heat as Ajax pounded into her pussy harder. The headboard slammed against the wall and with each thrust, Imani's screams turned into mewling yelps of pleasure.

Imani whimpered as she felt herself drawing closer to climax. Ajax could see that she was getting close and he began to slow down his thrusting. Instead of hard and fast strokes, he began to plunge into Imani's pussy with slow and deep thrusts.

He allowed every inch of her tightness to clench around his cock so that the maximum amount of ecstasy could shoot through her body. Pleasure surged in potent waves through Imani's core.

Finally, she came. Hard.

"Yes... Yes Ajax!" Imani cried out.

Ajax grunted and then pulled his cock out of her immediately. Six spurts of his fluid landed on her belly as he came simultaneously with her.

They both lay there gasping for breath and reveling in the ecstasy they had just experienced. The thick spurts of cum on Imani's belly painted her once and for all as belonging to Ajax. He had claimed her as his mate in the most primal way.

Ajax cleaned both of them up and they hopped into the hotel room shower.

Together in the shower, they lathered each other down and spent time caressing and embracing underneath the steamy flow of water. A soothing finish to a hard day.

Imani was almost ready for round two. The only thing that prevented her from pouncing on Ajax a second time was the fact that they needed to call Franco. She'd kept him in the dark long enough as she reveled in her reunion with Ajax. She couldn't keep him there a minute longer.

Franco was still a gay man alone in the town that hated him. They still had secrets to uncover and based on the new information Imani had received, they were on the verge of uncovering something big. For environmental investigators, they were almost in over their heads. It was possibly what they'd found was even bigger than what Ajax thought it was.

Betrayal and fraud were one thing, but what if Franco had discovered something else.

They got dressed and lay in bed together a while longer. When she could no longer wait anymore, Imani picked up the phone and dialed Franco's number.

As usual, he picked up almost immediately once he saw that Imani was the one calling. She updated him on everything that they had found out. She told him that she had decided not to leave for New York and then she told Franco everything Ajax had said to her.

Franco took the information in but didn't give Imani much feedback. She could hear the wheels of his mind whirring even over the phone. Whatever Franco knew, whatever he refused to tell her, she had a strong feeling that it aligned very closely with what Ajax said.

Despite her revelation, Franco still didn't spill a thing. He made Imani promise that she would get to Homer as quickly as possible the next morning. Imani refused to move before the sun was up but she agreed to get there as soon as she could. After hanging up, she cuddled into bed next to Ajax.

The last thing she heard before going to bed that night was Ajax's voice whispering, "I love you."

She could listen to that lullaby forever.

The next morning they had a quick breakfast of some terrible bagels, cream cheese and lukewarm coffee. Imani didn't care too much about breakfast, she just wanted to get on the road. She had received a text message from Franco early that morning indicating he had survived the night. If she had been there, she wasn't sure he would be able to say that.

Homer was a terrifying place and she couldn't wait to be done with it. She had not confirmed with Ajax yet, but she had a feeling that if she wanted him to follow her out east he wouldn't put up too much of a fight. If his daddy went to jail, there wouldn't be that much out in Oklahoma worth standing still for.

He already knew Imani couldn't stay here. Ajax drove like the type of guy who'd grown up on Nascar races. The three hour drive was cut down into a solid two and a half hours. Imani was partly scared her life and partly scared that they'd pulled over by a dirty cop with an agenda and quotas to fill. But they made the drive safely.

Somehow, driving through Oklahoma with Ajax

was much different than driving there with anyone else. He'd point out high schools he'd played against, places where he'd gone on dates, the hometowns of people he'd known. Instead of a flat and boring place, Imani got the sense that someone had lived a life out here. Ajax breathed life into the state and she began to notice that it seemed less empty than she'd originally perceived it.

Once their car rolled into town, Imani felt the hairs on the back of her neck tense up. Ajax looked over at her and she knew he could tell just how scared she was. Visions of those terrifying men in white robes firing gun shots into the sky flashed into her mind. The blood rushed out of her pretty brown face.

"Listen... I've got you Imani, alright?" Ajax offered her words of comfort as he pulled into the motel parking lot.

Imani noticed Franco come out onto the porch. He waved down at them with a big cheery smile. He was really the type of guy that no one could get down, no matter how hard they tried. Ajax got of the truck and tried to urge Imani to get out. Her body refused to touch the door handle. Ajax walked around and opened the door, helping her out. She felt sick to her stomach the moment her feet touched the pavement.

By the time she was on the ground, Ajax had made his way down the stairs. He was dressed for work with a big smile on his face.

"Well I'm glad to see y'all."

Ajax half-smiled and Imani rushed to hug Franco. She realized in her attempts to escape, she hadn't just been a bitch to Ajax, she'd abandoned Franco too. She would have never forgiven herself if something had happened to him in Homer.

Franco released her from his hug and then said solemnly, "I'm afraid we'll have to head out to your dad's ranch Ajax."

"Lester?"

Franco nodded.

"Some of what we found was massive amounts of pollution from the paper plant but there was something else too. Something usually found in decomposition."

"Like animals or something?" Ajax said.

Franco shook his head, "Human."

Ajax's face turned pale.

"We're supposed to wait for the feds to get here."

"The feds will take way too long. We should get the sheriff!" Ajax suggested.

Imani and Franco exchanged glances. Ajax was

no dummy, but he could be painfully naive about how things worked in Homer.

"Ain't the sheriff and your paw old friends?"

Ajax nodded.

"But it depends on what you find. The sheriff is a good man."

He could see that Imani and Franco were both skeptical.

"Don't worry y'all. We'll talk to Lester. If he's done something he ain't so stupid as to cross the sheriff. He'll turn himself in."

Franco replied, "What if he's armed and decides he's not going down without a fight."

"I know my father. Imani, trust me on this."

Imani had felt the hunk of metal under her feet in Ajax's truck. She had a feeling that he was a better sharpshooter than Lester, no matter how much more experience Lester had. If there was any trouble, she had a sense Ajax really could handle it.

"Why don't we just go talk to him."

"We should only have a few more hours 'til the FBI gets here anyways," Franco said, shrugging his shoulders.

Neither Imani nor Franco was particularly thrilled by the idea of confronting Lester. But Imani had a feeling that Ajax needed to do this. She shuddered as she thought about what Franco had said.

Human decomposition. That meant somehow, there were dead bodies on Lester's ranch. He'd either killed somebody or he knew someone who did. Neither option soothed Imani.

She got into Ajax's truck and Franco drove their rental all the way over to the Redford Ranch where Lester lived. Ajax got out of the truck and reached for another small handgun underneath the driver's seat. Jesus. Men out here really did love their guns. He holstered the gun on his hip and said to her, "Don't be scared. I promise, it'll be alright."

Imani wasn't sure she believed him, but she was already here. She had no choice. Ajax's whirlwind plan to get his father to turn himself in had suddenly become her reality.

The three of them approached the ranch house and knocked. No one answered. Ajax peered in through the window. No sign of Lester.

"He's not home?"

Ajax shrugged, "He's probably in the barn. His tractor's here so I'm guessing he ain't too far off."

The three of them wandered around to the barn. They could hear clanging and clattering through the door, suggesting that Lester was indeed behind the barn doors.

Ajax opened the door and his father looked up at

him surprised. He was even more surprised when he saw Imani and Franco trailing Ajax.

"Ajax. Silly name anyways. Old bat..." He mumbled.

Imani could smell the whiskey from the door. She looked at what Lester was doing and saw him polishing a decent sized hand gun much like the one Ajax had pulled out from underneath his driver's seat.

"Paw, I brought these scientists down here to ask you a few questions."

"Questions?" He grunted.

Franco and Imani looked at each other, each silently daring the other one to speak.

"Yeah. Questions. Franco?"

Franco cleared his throat. Usually, Franco could handle even the most tense situations. But seeing a nutty old farmer with Klan affiliations (and polishing a handgun at that) sent him into a state of anxiety unlike anything Imani had seen.

"Why don't you summarize it Ajax."

Ajax seemed fearless in the face of his father wielding a weapon. Imani knew it was the wrong time, but she couldn't help but admire his bravery. Or his foolishness.

"They're saying they found signs of pollution on the farm paw."

Lester grunted, "See...It's that damned factory just like I said..."

"You set it up. You set it up Lester to frame Chuck. Don't you fuckin' lie to me," Ajax said.

Imani could see his hand shaking, hovering over the holster on his hip. Her eyes widened. Ajax was mad. Really mad. All the years of living under his father's thumb had apparently gotten to him and this had been the final breaking point. Ajax was done keeping his daddy's secrets and he was clearly done defending him.

Lester began to put the gun's pieces back together. Imani was no expert in weapons, but she had a feeling things were going to go south quickly the instant Lester had a gun in his hand.

"If I did set it up... Well they deserve it. Chuck's a bloody cheat."

"Dad you're drunk."

"So what if I'm drunk."

"That ain't all these scientists found, you know that?"

Lester looked up. His reddened face began to turn ghost white.

"Wha'd'y'mean by that?"

"They found evidence of human decomposition in your soil."

"Must be the cows or somethin'."

"It wasn't bloody cows, paw. Tell me the truth."

His hand was now gripping the handle of the gun. Imani closed her eyes and hoped that she was in a nightmare. She'd just confessed her love of Ajax; the last thing she wanted was to see him pull a gun on his father and risk going to jail forever before they'd had a chance to really, properly be together. She prayed that Ajax's impulses wouldn't get the best of him.

"They're a bunch of bloody government liars..."

"No they aren't... You're the liar Lester... And I've thought this for a long time but now I'm going to ask you straight and I swear to God I'll put a fuckin' bullet in your brain myself if you lie... What happened to my maw Lester... Did you kill her."

Lester looked into his son's eyes and everyone standing in the room could see that he did it. Guilty men just wore the look on their face; it didn't take a genius or a courtroom to pronounce Lester guilty.

"I never harmed a hair on that woman's head," He slurred.

Ajax pulled out his gun and pointed it at his father.

"Ajax! No!" Imani shrieked.

Ajax ignored her and continued, "Tell me the truth. Tell me the truth paw!"

His hands trembled. Lester loaded up his gun with six bullets and then set it on the table.

"Put the gun down Ajax and I'll tell you the truth."

Ajax's hand hovered uncertainly for a moment but then he dropped his gun to the ground. Franco ran for it and Ajax didn't stop him.

"I killed her, okay? I was the one who did it... But it was an accident... I didn't meant to hurt her."

"Bastard! You're a fucking bastard!" Ajax screamed.

He was going ballistic. Face red. Tears streaming down. He screamed for his gun. Imani screamed, "No!" Lester picked his gun off the table and raised it. Imani closed her eyes, her heart throbbing in her chest. Franco and Ajax both stared wide-eyed as Lester put the gun into his mouth and fired.

Bang!

Imani dropped to the ground.

Proposal

❧

I mani woke up and saw an ambulance. Her head was just clear enough that she figured out it wasn't for her. Before she could move or say anything, she felt Ajax's hand touch her.

"Imani... Imani are you alright?"

Franco was talking to the EMTs in the distance. She sat up and then nodded to Ajax. Fine. Sure, she was fine. As fine as one could be after watching a man put a gun in his own mouth and fire. Imani's stomach turned and she thought she was going to be sick. She clutched at Ajax's shirt and mumbled, "I'mgonnabesick..."

He ran off and returned with an empty basin that had the residual smell of cow manure. Imani threw up. Then she dry heaved in front of the basin a while longer. She saw the ambulance peeling off out of the corner of her eye and then Franco returned by her side.

Ajax and Franco helped Imani to her feet.

"You okay?" Franco asked.

Imani nodded. Emptying the contents of her stomach somehow made her feel better.

"You've been out for like ten minutes," Ajax added, "Why don't we take you inside, get you cleaned up."

"The police are still over there, I've got to give a statement," Franco said, "I'll tell them where you guys are going and they'll get your statements after."

Imani and Ajax nodded and then Imani leaned on Ajax as they made their way to the ranch house. Imani never thought she'd find herself inside this house again. Her legs still felt weak beneath her as she balanced her weight on Ajax. He thrust the door open to the downstairs powder room and gave Imani a rinse for her mouth in a small Dixie Cup. She washed her face afterwards and then turned to Ajax.

"Are you okay?" She asked.

Ajax shrugged.

"I don't know if it's hit me yet. He was alive when the medics got here."

"Then we should go to the hospital."

Ajax shook his head.

"I can't. He killed my mother Imani... I knew they used to fight... I remember being younger and hearing 'em fight... I suspected later on he used to hit her but... I don't know if I can forgive him Imani..."

She nodded.

"Then what do we do now?"

"We head outside and we talk to the cops. That's all we can do."

"Okay."

Imani walked up to Ajax and gripped his hand tightly as they walked outside. They'd all just seen something horrendous and there was this sensation amongst the three of them of being shell-shocked. Each of them felt like they were play-acting as characters in a movie. They spoke to the cops, repeating their statements in shaky, shell-shocked voices.

The mystery of what had been happening in Homer, Oklahoma was solved. But for someone standing at a point of resolution, Imani didn't feel very good. Once they were done speaking to the cops, Franco packed his things and they all drove out of town to the motel close to the airport where Ajax and Imani had recently spent the night.

None of them were interested in another night in Homer. Once they got there, Franco called their boss. In five days, they could fly out back east. Once the boss had been filled in, he'd instantly put them on a small, paid leave.

In the middle of the night, Ajax got a call. His father had survived. Drunk off his ass, his aim had been just a little bit off. The doctor's believed they could save him. Ajax promised them he'd come into the hospital the next day, but he wasn't sure he could stand the sight of his father after what he'd found out.

The next morning, Imani and Ajax woke up in a somber mood. Even if Imani was technically on vacation, she felt anything but relaxed. Ajax called out of work but left early in the morning anyways. Imani didn't bother asking, but she had a feeling that he was headed to the hospital to spend time with his father.

Franco came over to Imani's suite with a bacon, egg and cheese bagel from the local donut shop. Again, nothing could compare to the New York bagels that Imani was used to, but at least it numbed the gnawing hunger in Imani's belly. She and Franco sat at the foot of her bed and ate quietly.

"Doing okay today?"

Imani shook her head.

"No... Yesterday we watched a guy shoot himself in the face. That wasn't in the job description."

"But at least you have Ajax, right?"

Imani sighed. Yes, she had Ajax. But there was still a limited amount of time before she'd have to go back East. There was no guarantee that her relationship with Ajax would be anything more than a fling. They'd said that they loved each other but that was it. It still felt premature for Imani to bring up plans for the future. As much as she cared for Ajax, as much as they'd been through together, she still wasn't comfortable asking him to uproot his entire life to come to the East Coast.

"Technically. I just have no idea where things are going with us."

"He's not like Brian. You know that, right?" Franco said.

Imani raised an eyebrow. After years of Franco's negative comments about Brian, she thought it was just in his nature to hate all the men she brought home. Imani couldn't help but feel curious about what exactly had swayed Franco's opinion of Ajax.

"Why do you say that?"

"I can tell. He's a good guy and he cares about you. If you want him once you're out of this hell hole... you shouldn't be afraid to tell him."

"Well thanks for the sage wisdom."

"You know, it's kind of my thing," Franco replied with a cheeky wink.

They finished their food and then Franco left Imani's room to go get a shower. Imani considered taking a walk around this new town, but she decided against it. Still tired from the day prior, she opted for lounging in bed and flipping through an old issue of Vogue she'd bought at the airport on the way to Oklahoma, but never read.

It was early afternoon before Ajax returned. He seemed upbeat. Imani found that a little odd. His father was in the hospital, most likely in a fight for his life. His reaction was unusual for a guy who's father was on the brink of death. But then again, most people's fathers hadn't also killed their mother's. Imani had known Ajax was sensitive about the subject of his mother. It was one thing to believe she was still alive and somewhere out there, but finding out she was dead must have shaken him to his core.

"Had a good morning?" She asked.

"Sure did. Glad to see your face," Ajax said, pulling Imani close and kissing her on the lips.

"What have you been up to?" He asked.

"Just reading in bed, trying to unwind. How was the hospital?"

"Fine. He's fine... Well... He will be... I guess..."

Imani found that hard to believe, but she could see that Ajax didn't want to talk too much about whatever he'd been up to.

"Kiss me," He said.

Imani tiptoed up to Ajax's lips and kissed him. Warm. Sweet. Everything that she didn't want to leave behind in Oklahoma. Imani wriggled out of his grasp awkwardly, knowing that she couldn't avoid this subject much longer.

"What's going to happen to us Ajax?"

"What do you mean?"

"Come on! We can't dance around this issue much longer. In a few days I'm going back to New York and I have no idea where this is going or what's going to happen between us."

"Well... We can be together if you want."

"So long distance? How are we supposed to make that work? I've never even seen you use a phone Ajax! I mean... and long distance never works! I just want to be sure that —," Imani began to panic.

Ajax pressed his index finger to her lips whispering, "Shh..."

"I'm worried Ajax."

"I know you're worried. But I said that we could be together, if you wanted. I didn't say it had to be long distance."

"Are you serious?" Imani asked.

She tried to tone down her joy. The last thing she wanted to do was to get her hopes up and face another disappointment.

"Yes, I'm serious."

Ajax reached into his pocket and pulled out a small black box. He opened the box and got down on one knee. Imani looked down at the man she'd slowly fallen in love with upon arriving in Oklahoma. His face was shining with joy as he revealed the engagement ring he'd spent the morning picking out. Imani could feel tears welling up in her eyes.

"Imani," Ajax started, "I want to be with you. I will move across the country for you if you'd allow me to. Since I met you, my life has been different. The sun's been shining brighter in Homer ever since you came. I can't let you get away from me... Not when you're the only girl I've ever really loved... So please, will you marry me?"

Imani was surprised both my Ajax's confession and by his proposal, but she had no desire to say no to him. In fact, as she stared into Ajax's blue eyes and as she stared at the flawless diamond ring he'd bought her, she knew that this was right and this was what was meant to happen all along.

"Yes... Yes I'll marry you Ajax," Imani said.

Ajax took the ring and slipped it onto her finger. Imani held it up to the light filtering through the window and let out an unwilling squeal. Ajax stood up and engulfed her in his big, meaty arms. As Imani let herself relax in his embrace, he pulled her chin towards his face and kissed her lips.

"I love you Imani Raymond..."

"I love you too..."

"Go back east. I've got a few loose ends to tie up here, but I promise you, I'll be in New York before you know it."

"Promise?"

"I promise..."

"Maybe we should try to go somewhere besides New York..." Imani said.

"Yeah? What makes you say that?"

"I don't know... We're starting a new chapter of our lives. We could probably use the change of pace."

"We'll see babe... We'll see," Ajax replied, kissing Imani on the forehead once again.

Boston

It was strange not being in New York anymore. Boston wasn't exactly "foreign territory", but it was foreign enough to Imani. Starting over had its perks and its drawbacks. Imani missed working with Franco all the time. They still managed to see each other often, and all Imani had done was transfer branches of the company, so they could still talk about work all the time. It wasn't the same, but their friendship was still alive.

Boston was quieter than New York. There was still the bustle of a big city but still, Boston seemed quieter. The T was quiet. There were more quiet neighborhoods, and in general, Imani could feel the slower pace of the city. It was a far bigger adjustment for her husband, Ajax.

Ajax comprised of most of the perks of moving towns to Boston. In fact, moving out to Boston had been his idea. He couldn't stomach New York and Imani couldn't stomach another small town like Homer.

Ajax's financial situation had changed massively too. He had always made a cool six figures for managing his father's ranches, but then, Lester went to prison. Ajax's money had dried up for a short time. After a few months in prison, Lester Redford had passed away. His newlywed son — and perennial shame to Lester — had inherited all the money from all of his ranches. He'd had no time to change his will, though he'd had plenty of time to let Ajax know what he thought about him marrying a black woman.

The total value of all the land and ranches that Ajax inherited was over $12 million. Ajax then sold all the ranches except one in Homer, Oklahoma. He kept a few ranch hands and a manager to keep the place running. Although not all the memories in Homer, Oklahoma were good, they were still the clay that had formed Ajax's complicated life. Homer was still the place where he'd fallen in love with Imani, his beautiful wife.

Now that he had all the money he could ever need, and they were in a new, beautiful city, Ajax decided to try his hand at something different. He'd borrowed Imani's car and driven about an hour outside of Boston, to this small town named Ayer, Massachusetts. Out there, he'd bought a dairy farm from an elderly couple on the verge of retirement.

Ajax could never fully leave his life as a country boy behind. The farm's profits had been dwindling over the years, but if Ajax could run a ranch in a town with about 1,000 people, he was sure he could revitalize an East Coast dairy farm. So he'd set about doing that while his beautiful wife continued to work to save the world one day at a time.

On a Friday, Ajax returned home at seven in the evening and found Imani waiting for him over the stove. She could make a mean roast chicken and she cooked rice in that fancy way you sometimes saw in Japanese restaurants. Ajax couldn't have been happier to have made her Mrs. Redford.

Shotgun weddings weren't unusual in Homer, but he could tell that Imani had been surprised at his willingness to tie the knot. Ajax had known Imani was the woman he wanted to spend the rest of his life with from the first time they'd made love. Everything about her was different from what was "usual" in Homer, from her rich skin tone, to the elegant way she carried herself.

Ajax was glad he didn't wait a minute longer to

propose. Hell, in a town where most of the girls are taken by the time they reach their eighteenth birthdays, you learn that waiting around for love is more often than not, a huge mistake.

Sometimes you have to dive headfirst into love and just have faith that things will work out alright.

"Good evening Mrs. Redford," He called to her as he walked through the foyer of the townhouse into the kitchen.

Imani smiled once she saw Ajax. Her husband seemed to grow more attractive to her every day. His skin had lost the tiniest bit of its tan but his blue eyes still shone with excited fervor.

"Hey, I got done with work early so I figured I'd start cooking."

"It smells delicious."

"Really?"

Ajax nodded and walked over to Imani, engulfing her in a strong-armed hug from behind. She rested her head on Ajax's shoulders as she hugged him, wrinkling her nose as he got a little too close. He smelled a little too strongly of damp earth and cows.

"You're a little stinky," She giggled, pulling away.

Ajax kissed her on the cheek, "You like it... I

know you do. It's all a big fantasy to you right? You get the city life and the guy who works with his hands. I'm not one of those East Coast yuppies."

"You mean hipsters?"

"Is that what we're calling 'em these days."

'Go take a shower and then come down to dinner!" Imani called.

Ajax bounded upstairs to their shower and stripped down to nothing. His body hadn't changed much since moving to the East Coast. He still got to work with his hands and all the tough, outdoors work kept all his muscles perfectly chiseled without sacrificing their natural, sculpted look.

Ajax hopped into the shower and felt his dick stiffen as the hot water ran down his back. He was thinking of Imani. This always happened when he thought about his wife. Ajax couldn't wait to get her into the bedroom after their dinner. After he showered, Ajax slipped into a comfortable pair of grey sweatpants and a white v-neck t-shirt. His dick bulged through the sweatpants as he walked downstairs.

He couldn't figure out how she'd worked that fast, but Imani had laid out a whole spread on the dining table. Roast chicken, rice, sweet potatoes, and a heaping pile delicious steamed vegetables.

Not only that, but Imani had poured two tall glasses of red wine for them. Ajax loved the dry flavor of Shiraz. Out in the West, beer had been his drink of choice.

Mrs. Redford had introduced him to some of the finer things in life.

They sat together and started eating. At first, they ate in silence. Ajax kept stealing glances at Imani as if he were in a high-school cafeteria, sneaking a glance at his older, off-limits crush. Finally, Imani noticed her husband's eyes boring into her across the table.

"So you're not gonna say anything? Just stare?"

Ajax winked. He had a lot planned for Imani after dinner, more than she realized.

"Maybe I will just stare..."

"Oh hush," Imani chuckled, "Tell me about work today?"

"Great. Bess and Molly gave birth to two calves. Milk sales are up and the petting zoo portion of the farm is almost completely built."

"That's excellent!"

"I know I can turn things 'round on that old farm. If we could strike gold in Homer, we can do it here."

Imani nodded. Ajax's shrewdness with money

was growing more attractive to her as time passed. For the first time in her life, she didn't have to worry about money. Imani made plenty of money on her own but nothing beat the added security of knowing that her husband was successful too.

Ajax asked, "What about you? How's work?"

Imani sighed, "It's going well but there's a whole slew of office politics going on right now. We won't be able to get a move on the Maine Farmer's Project until October."

"Jeez."

Ajax and Imani looked at each other across the table. Through silent communication, they realized that neither of them wanted to be talking about work — not when the bedroom was waiting.

They finished up quickly. Ajax washed the dishes and Imani rinsed. The tedious married couple's ritual became fraught with tension due to their desire for each other. Ajax stole glances at Imani, watching her perky breasts heave as she breathed while sliding a plate under the running water.

Imani caught glances at her husband too. She watched Ajax's super-sized muscles bulging and contracting as he washed up. Even doing the most regular activities, Ajax managed to exude alluring appeal.

Once they were done, Imani began to coyly make her way to the bedroom. Before she was too far out of reach, Ajax grabbed her arm and squeezed tightly.

"No," He said, in his deep, commanding voice.

Imani turned to look at him with uncertainty.

"Right here, right now," Ajax said.

And that was all he had to say. It had been a long time since they'd had sex outside of the bedroom. From the look on Ajax's face, Imani could tell he was feeling kinky. He hoisted her up onto their kitchen counter. Imani flashed back to the time they'd first made love. She flashed back to what it was like when Ajax was a stranger, and love making included awkward fumbling and guesswork.

Now that he knew exactly where to touch her and how to touch her, making love had grown sweeter and more addictive. Everyone had predicted a dip in love-making in their relationship but as time passed, their passion for each other blazed deeper and hotter than ever before.

Imani looked into her husband's eyes, begging him not show her any mercy with her silent gaze.

Ajax pressed his lips to Imani's and as his plump lips made contact with hers, she instinctively stuck her tongue into Ajax's mouth. His lips tastes sweet — sweeter than any other man's. And just like a drunk, her lips touching his initiated the point of no return. Imani grabbed at Ajax's chest, pulling him closer to her by the shirt. With her legs wide open and him standing between them, they were clothed actors in the dress rehearsal for a nudie scene.

Ajax pressed his hands to Imani's back and felt her heart racing and her skin growing hot with desire beneath his palms. She was burning, burning with desire for him, the same desire that broiled between his loins, pushing him ever forward. Ajax peeled off Imani's shirt and those beautiful, voluptuous breasts he so loved swung into view.

Some men would try to convince you that the excitement wore off once you knew what you were getting with a woman. But Ajax found the opposite to be true. His excitement palpitated in his loins and his dick thrust eagerly against his cotton boxer briefs.

Ajax moved his head down to Imani's breasts and kissed each one outside her bra. His hand slithered to the three hooks that cinched her bosom tightly into place and in one swift motion, he removed her brassiere and tossed it onto the ground. The instant her nipples made contact with the cool air of the kitchen, they stood like hardened bullets. Their robust, dark brown color was almost purplish and they called to Ajax like darkened black-berries, begging him to run his tongue over them and take her entire breast into his mouth.

Imani braced herself against Ajax's throbbing chest as he moved to kiss her on the lips again. Her fingers tip-toed down the length of his body and hovered just around his belt. She could feel the heat from his lustful cock even as her hand dangled dangerously over his zipper.

"Pull it out babe," He whispered into her ears.

She needed no further encouragement. Imani saw the outline of his dick through his grey sweat-pants. Even with the obfuscation of his size from the pants, Ajax's dick bulged forward ferociously. She pulled the grey, woolen sweatpants to the ground, keeping her gaze locked onto her prize. His dick seemed to be breathing in the same quick rhythm as his heart. Ajax gasped as Imani's hand touched his dick through his boxers. She slipped his pants to the ground, then his boxers.

Ajax's thick cock was exposed to the cool air and he stood hard and fully ready to plunge between Imani's thighs. Imani slipped her cute, thigh hugging shorts to the side and Ajax moved in closer like a shark lunging in for the kill. His blue eyes hypnotized her into submission, as they always did.

Memories from the past of hundreds of hundreds of instants of glorious lovemaking heightened their anticipation to a fever pitch.

Imani could practically feel her ears ringing with desire. Her face was flushed. Her pussy was dripping and growing wetter and wetter as Ajax's predatory member moved closer.

She gasped as she felt his cock touch her entrance for the first time. Ever since they'd started making love skin-on-skin, everything started to feel much better. Imani didn't know how to describe it, but there was something almost magical about feeling every inch of Ajax as he thrust into her. There was something drunken and lascivious about allowing him to coat the walls of her wetness with his sticky fluid.

Ajax began to press his dick deep into Imani. Dinner and dishes had been their foreplay. Imani gasped as Ajax's thickness stretched apart her tight entrance. She clenched her pelvic floor muscles, allowing Ajax a slow, tight entry between her legs. Ajax grunted as he slipped his cock into her inch by inch. Imani spread her legs wider, breathing slowly as he finally inserted his monstrous dick fully into her pussy.

Now she and Ajax were joined at the hips. His

lips grazed her ear and he clutched her body tightly, gripping her right at her ass cheeks. He was so close to her that his scent colonized her nostrils. His masculine scent numbed her like a few too many margaritas, making her dizzy with desire. Imani gasped as Ajax started to move his dick within her. Tonight, everything was a climax of its own.

His thrusting began slowly. As his dick squeezed between her folds, rubbing ever inch of both her outer and inner lips, Imani could sense her body responding to him against her will. She craved a slow pace, she craved the heat of Ajax's body pulsing beneath her finger tips. She craved the sensation of the hot blood rushing to his tool, throbbing inside of her as he plunged in and out in a divine rhythm.

Imani cried out as Ajax's hardness plunged just a tad too deep. The sharp shooting pain did nothing to overpower the strong sensations of pleasure that were engulfing her. Ajax thrust into her harder and harder. Imani's pussy grew wetter and pleasure began to swirl inside her like a hurricane. Lubrication slipped around Ajax's cock, making it easier for him to slide in and out of his wife's tight little hole.

His skin, ramming unceasingly into her tight, hot little hole felt too damned good. Ajax hungered to coat her walls with his seed, to fill her belly up with his child. Ajax craved breeding her, then watching her grow thicker and thicker in the months after he seeded her. Just the thought stiffened his cock and forced an eager grunt from his throat.

"Yes..." Imani whispered.

He wanted to hear her mewl in bliss.

"You like that?" Ajax grunted.

"Yes..." Imani breathed, focusing her attention to the cock that was plunging in and out of her furiously. Ajax was beginning to sweat, as was she. His tanned skin glowed in the evening light and his muscles grew sexier as the slick sweat covered them in a thin coat.

"Whose pussy is this?" Ajax growled in her ear.

"Yours..." Imani whispered.

Ajax raised his hand to her throat, but didn't clasp his hands around it, saying, "Yours who?"

Imani loved the feeling of his hand touching her throat so tenderly. She knew what he could do. She knew that while he was pummeling her with his big, hard, cock, he could really hurt her, squeezing his hand around her throat until she answered him. But he didn't. He just threatened her with another level of domination — and he knew she would comply. Imani delighted in this just as much as he did.

"Yours daddy... It's yours..."

Imani and Ajax both felt her pussy clamping

tighter around his cock and his cock growing even stiffer inside her as she said the "magic words". Ajax was just possessive enough that he needed to hear her say them. He needed to know that he'd claimed her. She was his and his alone.

He began to pound into her faster and faster, approaching climax, but mentally preparing for a second (and third, and fourth, and maybe a fifth) round of love-making. Life had grown busy all around them, but the hearth-fire in the bedroom still burned, deep and bright orange like coals.

"Harder!" Imani moaned.

As Ajax thrust into her gaping depths, Imani convulsed and quivered. The release that began in her pussy didn't end there. She felt her legs tense up and wrap Ajax's body close to hers. The flesh on her thighs mercilessly clung to Ajax's flesh despite the sticky layer of sweat between the two of them. Then Imani's wetness throbbed in slow waves. With each wave, her skin seemed to be lit ablaze. She moaned. And moaned. And Ajax held her close, still for a moment, feeling her beautiful womanly body convulsing around his cock.

Once her long, multi-orgasmic climax was finished. She was quivering, quiet, but still bucking her hips forward, eager for more.

"Let's move it to the bed," Ajax whispered into her ear.

Imani nodded weakly. She wrapped her arms around Ajax's thick neck, clinging to him like a koala to a tree. He kept his spent wife embedded firmly on his cock and then hoisted her off the counter. She wrapped her arms around him more tightly and her breasts undulated as he moved her towards the bedroom.

Imani had been in charge of picking the sheets here. While Ajax's rustic, western decor peppered some areas of the room, the bed was solely Imani's choosing. Silvery grey silk sheets provided a pampered sleeping experience and an even more erotic love-making experience. Ajax slipped his cock out of Imani, causing her to gasp loudly. He lay her back gently on the bed and stood above her for a few moments, eyeing her body, eyeing her throbbing pussy that lay engorged and excited for more.

"Touch yourself," Ajax commanded.

Imani started to slip her hands slowly down towards her pussy, uncertain of whether or not she wanted to obey him. Touching herself was fine, she didn't mind putting on a show, but now, she didn't want to touch herself, she wanted to feel her husband's cock spurting inside her over and over again as she shuddered in pleasure. Ajax teased her intentionally.

"I said... touch... yourself..." He repeated slowly, in a tone that told Imani resistance would be futile.

Her hand snaked down towards her clit. Imani shivered as her finger first brushed against her clit. After that orgasm, sensitive couldn't begin to describe it. She began by swirling her thumb around her clit in slow circles. She gasped if she even got close to touching her hardened nub directly. Imani spread her legs wider and closed her eyes as she rubbed herself.

She could feel Ajax's blue eyes boring into her, deriving pleasure from drawing out their encounter. If she could surmount the impatience, the reward of a deep climax would be more than worth it.

"Ohhh!" Imani started to moan.

"Very good. Put one finger inside yourself," Ajax commanded.

She obeyed, slipping an index finger into her sopping heat. Imani found her g-spot fast and started to rub her finger up and down the tender area with each motion. A thumb kept resting near her clit.

"Two fingers," Ajax demanded simply.

She added a second finger tenderly, as if she were terrified of what the increased arousal would beget. Imani closed her eyes and sucked air in quickly between her teeth. It was good. So, so good. She loved how Ajax taunted her. She loved showing him every bit between her legs. He was her husband... this show was for him and only him. And she loved feeling like his minx, his naughty secret and his bashful, blushing bride all at once.

"Yes... yes..." She moaned.

Imani's two fingers stretched her pussy slightly, adding tension to the sensual up and down rubbing against her g-spot. She could feel climax boiling inside her, but she refused to let herself release until she received Ajax's command — or until his prick rested between her legs again.

Ajax considered himself patient enough, but the scene before him was hard to resist. His beautiful, put-together wife was mewling as she fingered herself. She looked so hot and so absolutely delicious. He moved into bed and threw her legs up over her head. Her pussy bulged forward, a swollen hot slit, begging for more stimulation than it had already received.

Ajax thrust his cock into her fast, like he was going down a slide. And slide he did. Imani groaned as he pushed deep inside her.

"Yes..." She gasped, "Harder..."

She whispered "harder" almost meekly, as if she

were terrified to ask Ajax to plunge deeper into her. Imani clutched the bed sheets and Ajax began to pound into her hard and fast. Before, he'd been teasing her, but now he wanted to cum. He hungered to coat the walls of Imani's sopping wet pussy with his seed and she wanted to do absolutely nothing to stop him.

"Harder..."

Sweat thickened on both of their skin. Imani looked into Ajax's blue eyes as he breathing grew shallow. She relaxed and then she came — long and hard. Imani groaned and gasped, clawing at Ajax's ass and back as she released. Her pussy clenched and then unclenched repeatedly around his cock, attempting to milk him dry as she orgasmed.

As Imani quivered there limp, Ajax continued to thrust. She was spent from her climax, and he was about to be spent from his. He pounded into her hard, gritting his teeth as he thick hardness disappeared between her legs. Ajax let out one final growl when he was finished. His dick twitched three, four, five times as huge jets of his cum lined his wife's walls. Imani shuddered beneath him.

Ajax gasped for breath. He pulled out of Imani and immediately rolled over onto his back. Both on their backs, their hands snaked towards each other. Their fingers found a home in each other and they both breathed, hard and deep, trying to come back down to earth.

When they did, they lounged in each other's arms for a while and then fell asleep. Their breathing was always syncopated once they'd made love. Tonight was no different — at least in that regard.

*

The next week, Imani had a few days off, and Ajax had to head out to the farm in Ayer. She made him breakfast and then kissed him good-bye. Imani rarely had time at home alone and while she missed Ajax, she relished that alone time. Her phone rang. An alert in her calendar — period start day.

But her period never arrived that day.

*

Her brand new box of tampons remained untouched a few days after.

*

It was two weeks after Imani's predicted "period start day" and she was starting to get nervous about Aunt Flo's arrival. She wasn't the type to miss the bus, let's just say. Aunt Flo was as regular as Christmas, and predictable. Imani had never had a pregnancy scare before. And now, she wasn't sure she would have even considered this a "scare".

It would be a surprise — although it shouldn't

have been — but it wouldn't be a scare. She and Ajax had talked loosely about having a baby for a while but they had never planned anything. They'd just been less careful. Imani calculated the time since they'd been the least careful. It hadn't been her exact ovulation day, but she didn't really know her exactly ovulation day outside of a guess, so it was entirely possible.

Pregnant.

Imani never thought she'd see the day. She thought back to when she was studying for her PhD program and she thought herself to be "old" to be a mother. Back then, she'd been comparing herself to women from her old neighborhood. Back there, you were an old mother if you were a day older than twenty-eight. Imani had always needed a new measuring stick.

The question burned in her mind of whether she should find confirmation first, or tell Ajax. Would he be happy, or would he want more planning. Hints of insecurity that had been birthed in previous relationships began to rise to the surface. What if she had projected her desire of a child onto Ajax. What if that's not what he wanted at all. Then what?

She knew that Ajax would never leave her. But she'd also thought the same thing about Brian. That mistake still haunted her, even if thinking of Brian's name turned her stomach. No amount of showers could wash away what Brian did to her, the way he emotionally violated her all the years she'd been with him.

But Ajax wasn't like that. Right? There was no way she'd made the same mistake twice. Even if it was a weekend, Ajax was up in Ayer for the morning. Once of his mares was giving birth and he wanted to be there to help bring her into the world. Imani suited up to go outside. A simple pregnancy test would set her right. If it was nothing, it was nothing. And if she was about to have a baby, then she'd have to find some way to announce it to her husband.

She walked down to the drugstore, feeling like she was hiding a secret that not even she knew. Once she got there, Imani bought a bright pink box that promised the fastest results. She couldn't see what the rush was. Once you were pregnant, you were pregnant. No hurry there. The baby would come soon enough.

Back home, Imani grappled with whether she should find out now, or wait until her husband got home. Then she thought about the awkwardness of Ajax waiting impatiently outside the door for her to finish urinating on a stick. Imani decided to skip the discomfort and find out on her own. She closed her bathroom door and skimmed the instructions on the box. How hard could it be?

She eased out of her pants and hovered over the toilet as she coated the stick with some of her urine. Imani capped it and set it on the counter, washing her hands furiously as she waited. Each minute seemed to draw out slowly and her thoughts raced more and more. If she was pregnant, how would she be able to keep her job? Would Ajax help her with the baby? Would she have to go shopping for baby clothes? What about schools? In some parts of New England, the best private preschools had two year long wait lists.

Imani couldn't have counted down the minutes any faster. She paced around her bathroom. She stared into her bathroom mirror aimlessly. Finally, time was up. If she was pregnant, she'd know.

Imani flipped over the stick.

Not pregnant.

Wait, or did the little symbol mean pregnant?

Imani fished for the box in her bathroom trash can and then re-read the label on the back. Nope. She was wrong — and most definitely pregnant.

Pregnant with Ajax's baby. A welcome surprise for any new couple. Imani couldn't figure out why she still felt so uncertain. A part of it had to be the wounds from her past. Even if he'd been long gone, the insecurity that Brian had planted in her still lingered. Most people couldn't understand, except those who'd experienced a broken heart. Except those who'd experienced a man who whispered silver-tongued lies into your ear just to get you to ply to his will.

Imani threw the pregnancy test in the trash. She'd have a long wait at home before she could tell Ajax. And then, Imani wasn't sure if you were supposed to be ceremonious about this things. It was a cause for celebration but the clinical nature of the pregnancy test didn't thrust her into the party mood.

Imani cleaned up the house. She caught up on work. She messaged Franco that she had "big news" without revealing what it was. As she cleaned, Imani couldn't help but notice her wedding ring more than usual. She'd never expected to be married, but here she was, in love.

Marriage hadn't healed all the problems in the world like many had led her to believe it would. She was still the same person. Her past could still hurt her. Her future was still speckled with uncertainty. But there was something sacred and beautiful about the way she shared her life with Ajax. The ring, her bond, it all meant so much to her. Imani was ready to take the scary next step forward and plunge into the world of being a mother.

When Ajax got home, he was visibly tired and Imani didn't bother filling his head with the Big News just yet. She set dinner down for him, carefully avoiding their evening tradition of having a half glass of wine together each. No more wine for nine months. Already, everything was about the baby.

Ajax didn't seem to notice the absence of wine. He wolfed down his spaghetti — one of his Oklahoma favorites that Imani added pizzazz to — and then talked at length about his plans for the upcoming season and the pending financial success of the farm. As he ate, Ajax noticed that Imani was shifting uncomfortably. She had something on the tip of her tongue but she was too shy to share it.

"What's goin' on?" Ajax asked.

"Huh?" Imani had been spaced out thinking about baby cribs.

"I can tell when your mind is a million miles away."

Imani sighed, "I've been waiting all day to tell you..."

"Don't tell me we have to go to another ballet..."

"No, not another ballet."

"Then what?"

"I'm pregnant Ajax."

"You're playin'."

"Nope. I'm pregnant. 100% pregnant. My period is late, and I checked today."

Ajax turned to Imani with a big smile. His reaction wasn't excessively negative or positive. He was calm, and beaming from within with a glow that Imani recognized. He was happy, plain and simple.

"A baby... Wow... So we're really gonna do this huh?" Ajax said.

Imani nodded. Having a baby would be scary, but it was definitely what she wanted. Ajax seemed to understand. He stood up and pulled Imani to her feet. She rested her head on her big, strong husband's chest and his thick arms wrapped around her. His love engulfed her and the steady throbbing of Ajax's dull heart beat reassured her that this was what they both wanted.

"Do you think it'll be a girl or a boy?" Ajax asked.

Imani wasn't sure. She knew some women could tell from the moment they found out they were pregnant. But now, she wasn't so sure. She held onto Ajax and tried to see if she could find some internal sense.

But there was none. Imani was just happy to be having a child, it was almost like the gender of the baby didn't matter at all.

"I don't know," She replied, keeping her head softly pressed to Ajax's chest.

"Well whatever it is, boy or girl, we'll love 'em all the same right?" He asked.

Imani nodded and whispered, "Yes."

Standing there, holding Ajax in her arms, she couldn't believe just how far they'd come.

THE END

Sign up to get a text message notification when my next book drops:

https://slkt.io/qMk8

About Jamila Jasper

The hotter and darker the romance, the better.

That's the Jamila Jasper promise.

If you enjoy sizzling multicultural romance stories that dare to *go there* you'll enjoy any Jamila Jasper title you pick up.

Open-minded readers who appreciate **shamelessly sexy romance novels** featuring black women of all shapes and sizes paired with smokin' hot white men are welcome.

Sign up for her e-mail list here to receive one of these **FREE hot stories**, exclusive offers and an

update of Jamila's publication schedule: bit.ly/
jamilajasperromance

Get text message updates on new books: https://
slkt.io/gxzM

A Preview

Sample these chapters from my Amalfi Coast
Brotherhood Italian mafia romance series while you wait
for the next mafia romance series.

If you enjoy dark & twisted mafia romance stories, you
can binge the entire completed series on your eReader.

Enjoy the free chapters.

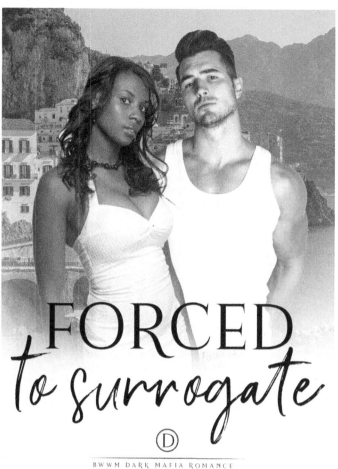

FORCED
to surrogate

Ⓓ

BWWM DARK MAFIA ROMANCE

the amalfi coast mafia brotherhood #1

JAMILA JASPER

Description

The last thing Jodi remembered was a shot of tequila.

Next thing she knows,
Italian sociopath Van Doukas has her chained in his basement...
And he's claiming she agreed to become the mother of his child.

There's a detailed contract and everything... with her signature.
Jodi will do whatever it takes to get away from him...
But she doesn't count on the 6'7" Italian Stallion being skilled with his tongue and excellent in bed.

Series Titles

Forced To Surrogate
Forced To Marry
Forced To Submit

Content Awareness

dark bwwm mafia romance

This is a mafia romance story with dark themes including potentially triggering content, frank discussions and language surrounding bedroom scenes and race. All characters in this story are 18+. Sensitive readers, be cautioned about some of the material in this dark but extremely hot romance novel. The character in this story is **forced by circumstance** into her situation.

Enjoy the steamy romance story...

Produce A Pure Italian Heir

VAN DOUKAS

There aren't enough cigarettes in the world for meetings with my father. The boss. Tonight, I meet with him to discuss something 'very important'. He calls everything 'very important', but tonight, I know exactly what he wants from me.

He wants me to kill again, this time for my foolish sister, who can't seem to keep herself out of trouble. Everyone in the family heard about what happened to Ana by now. That idiot Jew was foolish enough to put his hands on her with witnesses and expect nothing to happen? That's not how the Doukas family works, which he'll soon learn.

You mess with the Doukas family, we retaliate. If the Jew had any wits about him, he would disappear from the Amalfi Coast and head for the mountains or Sicily, or somewhere we don't have ears. He could go to Albania like Matteo. Maybe then we wouldn't find him. But fuck, I don't want to carry out another hit. Why can't that lazy fuck Enzo do it? Or better yet, Eddie. I carried out my first hit when I was two years younger than him. We spoil the new generation and wonder why our family falls apart.

None of this would be my responsibility if Matteo would get over himself and come down off his fucking mountain.

I stop my motorcycle and approach my father's front door. The all white old European style mansion sits on an excessive and opulent lot on the coast, right above the cliffs with a long path to the beach, a 'fuck you' to the tax collectors and the government who want to stop us from doing business.

Most of my siblings still live here, but I prefer keeping myself far away from papa and his... associates.

I can hear the party from the entrance. Seriously? On a fucking Tuesday afternoon? I assumed he called this meeting because he was working for once. He's intertwined in a different business based on the noise filtering outside. Please, Lord, let me not walk in on my father having sex with a model... *again*.

I open the front door to our old family home

without knocking and immediately regret it when a completely naked foreign woman runs giggling toward the door, too high and drunk to feel self-conscious, exposing her completely nude body to a stranger. At least I didn't find her twisted in bed with papa, although this isn't much better.

"Oh! Good afternoon, sir!" she teases me in crude Italian, spinning around to show off her assets. *Whore. Foreigner. Her tricks possess little interest to me.* My brothers Lorenzo and Matteo would sway more easily.

"Where's my father?"

She giggles and spins around again. Fucking hell, I wish the ground would swallow me up. My father's prostitutes do not interest me.

"Your papa?" she says, standing to face me with her legs slightly apart, daring me to ogle more of her body. I have no interest in whores and I want her to answer my fucking question.

Before I can answer, another one of my father's toys saunters into the foyer, naked. This one is young—she looks eighteen just about—far too young for my father. I grimace and keep my gaze firmly fixed away from the nude females. Just because the men in my family are bastards doesn't mean I have to follow suit.

If we don't conduct ourselves with respect, how can we expect the respect of the Amalfi Coast?

"Yes. My father. Sal," I grunt, failing to hide the irritation in my voice.

The woman ignores my irritated tone with her response.

"Oh, he's in the back with Boyka. I can take you there after we take you to bed upstairs."

How much is he paying these women? We're still struggling to get Jalousie off the ground and he spends all his money on Slavic hookers.

"Not interested. I have a meeting with him."

"Are you sure?"

I don't dignify them with a response. I walk past the girls, keeping my eyes away from their bodies. Where the hell is my father? I pass the long hallway with the family portraits and follow the loud music and the louder giggling from near the pool. The familiar sound of pool jets betrays papa's location.

He's in the fucking hot tub again, I know it. He spends all fucking day in the hot tub, dishing out orders and expecting work to happen without him lifting a fucking finger. It's a fucking miracle anything gets done around here.

My father chuckles loudly, and I brace myself before approaching him. He's the boss and you don't question the boss, even if he's your father and even if he cares more about partying and women than our family — than our future.

When I enter the back patio, the pungent smell of tobacco and marijuana surrounds me. Judging by the bottles of vodka on the ground, the piles of cigarette butts and the other piles of detritus, they've been at this fucking party since last night.

Fuck. I put the cigarette tucked behind my ear into my mouth and approach my father's outdoor speakers, unplugging them and stopping the little dance party happening around his hot tub. Three women, each wearing next to nothing with their tits out belly dance for him while he chuckles loudly, his fat stomach causing waves in the hot tub. When the music stops, they stop too and look up at me indignantly.

They don't have to ask who I am. The ones who don't know Van Doukas can tell that I'm related to Sal. I have my father's eyes, but thankfully, I don't have his overweight body or his bald head. The girls make booing sounds at me, but I brush them off.

"I'm here for our meeting," I say sternly to papa.

He chuckles and nods. "Yes. The meeting. I almost forgot."

Almost? He doesn't look like he's fucking prepared for a meeting.

Papa dismisses the girls, except for one —

Boyka. She slides into the hot tub next to him, twirling his thick plumes of chest hair around her fingers and sliding his freshly cut cigar between his lips. Nauseating. Papa coughs after a puff and taps the cigar over the edge of the hot tub.

"You're early."

"I'm twenty minutes late."

"Oh?"

"Papa, you said it was important. Shouldn't we conduct this business alone?"

None of the girls are dumb enough to rat on Salvatore Doukas, but unlike my father, I don't see the sense in taking risks.

Boyka's hand moves down my father's chest and I don't want to imagine what sorry shriveled part of him she touches next. I just want my orders so I can get the fuck out of this bachelor pad.

"I'm getting old, Van," he says. "I'm getting old."

He didn't call me down here to bitch about his old age. I furiously puff on my cigarette, waiting for him to get to the fucking point. Papa grunts as Boyka touches something... sensitive. Cristo...

Watching my father grunt through a hand job might be the only thing worse than watching him stick it to a woman.

"Do you mind postponing your fucking hand job until later?"

Boyka's hand rises guiltily from the water and I choke down bile. She really was touching the old fuck. I shouldn't swear at him or set him off. Papa might seem old, but he can have me killed. Any of my brothers would do it if he gave the command. Tread carefully, Van.

"Maybe I should leave," Boyka says, giving me a flirty glance as she plays with her tiny pink nipples.

"Yes," I snap. "Please get the fuck out of here."

Papa scowls. "Be respectful, Van. Boyka is a very dear—"

"I said please."

Papa smirks. "Boyka, return in thirty minutes. If we're not done..."

"We'll be done," I interrupt, glowering at my father. I don't have all afternoon for his games when I have the club to attend to.

Boyka reluctantly leaves.

"Are the women in this house allergic to fucking clothes?"

"None of them are allergic to fucking anything."

I'm not doing this with the old man today.

"Why did you call me here?"

I start another cigarette. I keep swearing I won't touch another, then I spend five minutes around papa and change my mind.

He leans back in the hot tub, displacing several

pints of water over the edge.

"I'm tired, Van," he groans, leaning back and rubbing his forehead.

"From working?"

My father doesn't pick up on the sarcasm. He hardly leaves his fucking hot tub anymore, and he hasn't done anything even remotely resembling working at either of the nightclubs, restaurants, apartment complexes or construction sites around town.

If it wasn't for me and Enzo, he wouldn't have the fucking time to boink Boyka or whatever the fuck he does with all these young Slavic women.

I still have to tread carefully around him. He's still my father, my boss, and I must obey him.

"Yes," he says, coughing. "From working. I need someone to take my place and lead the family soon. I want to retire, Van. You and I both know I need a break."

He spends every fucking day on vacation while his sons and nephews run his businesses. Vacation? We're the ones who need a fucking vacation.

"Perhaps you should contact Matteo about that."

My older brother spent his entire life preparing to be the boss. It's not my fault he fucked off, leaving his worthless children with us, I might add. I'm already halfway through my fucking cigarette and he hasn't closed in on the point.

Papa scoffs. "Matteo hasn't left Albania in four years. He left his children, his business, his fucking money, and he's not coming back. Give up on him."

"You're the one who trained him for the role. Send Enzo after him. Better yet, send his fucking son."

I don't want to go into the mountains to bring my jackass older brother back and I don't want to have this conversation with my father.

"Why don't you go to Albania?"

"Every time I'm in the same room as Matteo, he tries to kill me," I remind papa. I love Matteo, but he isn't exactly easy to get along with.

I'm surprised a woman tolerated him long enough to allow him to give her Eddie.

"Fair. But I need a replacement, Van. I don't want to be the boss anymore. I can't take the stress much longer."

Stress? What stress? Does my father seriously think sitting in his fucking hot tub banging whores counts as a job?

"Have you considered the role?" He asks before I can spew something disrespectful in my father's direction.

"Why would I want to be the boss of this fucking

family? It's filled with degenerates, fuck-ups, people who need more violence to be kept in line. I kill enough as it is. You don't want me to be the boss and nobody in this fucking family wants me as the boss."

"People respect you, Van."

"People fear me. There's a difference."

Papa nods. "Exactly. Personally, I think you would make a good boss."

"I disagree."

But I don't completely. Yes, the job would be horrific and I'd have even more blood on my hands than I do now by the end. I could bring honor back to our family, clean the streets of our scum, stop the Jews from fucking with our shit... but I can't. Not with Matteo gone. Even in the fucking Albanian countryside, he would find out what I did and Matteo would kill me.

"No," Papa replies calmly. "You don't. But I agree with your assessment that you're not quite ready."

"I never said that. I said I didn't want the job."

Nobody smart wants my father's job. He spent twenty years walking around with a target on his back before he built up enough trust, enough loyalty, enough captains in the streets of Italy to ensure his safety. I don't want to lose my freedom.

"You didn't have to say anything. I know my

son."

"Hm."

Arguing with my father is entirely senseless.

"You need an heir, Van."

"What?"

"I will give you the leadership of this family without the ritual, without the sacrifice and without the financial investment required. All I want is an heir."

"Why don't I go up to fucking Albania, then? Because I can't produce a child out of thin air."

Papa chuckles. "Don't you have women? If you want a woman... I filled this house with them. I have very young ones too. Eighteen. Nineteen. They make good mothers."

"I am not interested in fucking teenagers."

"Then find a whore like that old Greek Pagonis fuck. I don't care how you get the heir. You can prove how serious you are by giving me a child. I'll be generous. I'll give you a year."

"I don't want this role," I snap. "So the likelihood I'll produce an heir is slim."

Papa laughs, which only infuriates me further. There's nothing funny about bringing a child into the world.

"You can't lie to me, Van. You were always the most ambitious child. Maybe it's because you were smack in the middle and we didn't pay any attention to you. Who fucking knows?"

My father spent little time raising any of us, except for Enzo, and look how that fucking turned out.

"Thank you for the psychoanalysis."

Every time I visit my father, my desire for alcohol increases exponentially, along with my cravings for nicotine. He brings the worst out of everyone, especially me.

"No problem," he says, again ignoring my sarcasm.

"What happens if I don't produce an heir? Eh? You still need someone to take your place."

"I make this offer to Lorenzo if you don't produce what I want."

"What?" I would have at least expected him to mention one of our cousins, one of the very obedient captains from the northern coast, or even fucking Eddie, Matteo's 18-year-old son, would be better than my irresponsible fuck of a brother. That old fuck really knows me well because he just said the only thing that could get me to reconsider his stupid fucking offer.

"You heard me."

"Lorenzo would ruin this family. For fun."

"I know. And it would become your responsibility to save it. You would have to act as the boss to save Lorenzo from himself. You might as well earn the position."

Fuck this old man...

"I don't want a family life, papa. I don't want the fucking wife or the fucking family. I want this life. It's what I'm good at. Business. Killing. More killing. That's who you taught me to be."

I'm not a man who can picture himself kicking around a football with my children or taking them to the beach. I'm not built for seducing women for more than a night and dealing with the danger of introducing them to my life or worse, hiding it the way papa did with our mother.

He can pretend it's not his fault what happened to her, but we all know the truth. No woman deserves our life. I can't afford to react. He loves when he can draw a reaction out of me.

Papa continues, as if my reaction is irrelevant. "Part of this life means having a family. I can't expect my other children to carry on my bloodline."

"Matteo has a son. You have a fucking bloodline. Why don't you make him the fucking boss?"

"Eddie? Eddie will not survive long the way he lives."

"That's a way to talk about your grandson, eh?"

"Have another cigarette, Van."

I'm already on my fucking third. But I'm not in a position to turn down his offer, considering the shit he wants me to deal with right now. An heir? I thought he wanted me to kill someone. Producing an heir in a year... It's just fucking impossible. I stick the cigarette in my mouth and light it.

"You can't let the family fall apart. We aren't the only people who would suffer. What would happen to our people, good Italian people, when the only people around they can get money from are the fucking Jews, who hate our guts?" He says.

I can't let his guilt trip work on me.

"I want an heir."

"Hm."

"Consider what you would sacrifice by turning down my offer, Van. It's not just about the family. It's power. You act like you're a fucking saint, but you are my son. You enjoy power. You're just too much of a stuck up cunt to let yourself enjoy it."

"Thanks papa."

"You're welcome. Now, onto the matter of the Jew."

Fuck. I hoped my father would only piss me off one way today, but if we're discussing the matter of the Jew, I won't leave here tonight without an assignment. Someone else could easily do this job, but he wants me to kill. Because I'm good at it.

"I suppose none of my other brothers have the free time to do this?"

"I don't care. I need you to do it. The cunt offended this family."

"Perhaps we waste too much time retaliating for every offense. Ana told you to drop it."

I'm taking a risk just questioning his order, but he's pissed me off so much that I stopped caring.

"Decision making isn't women's work. It's our work. The man signed his own death warrant. I want it done soon. Call me when you finish the job."

"Hm."

"If you don't like the way I run this family, Van, you know what to do. I want to retire. Make an old man happy."

Drugs and whores are the only things that make my father happy.

"An heir," I scoff. "You want me to have a fucking bastard child to continue your bloodline? A bastard won't have any loyalty to his family. Children have a mother and a father, a mother they spend all their time with. If I fuck some poor woman, you won't have an heir. You'll have a problem on your hands."

"Then get creative. If you need to get the baby and kill the mother, do what you must."

What's happening to this family? When did we lose our way and talking about murdering women for our own ends? Papa... This life changed him. It was slow, but it changed him completely. Too bad there's no getting out.

"Thank you for the advice."

"You're welcome. Now get Boyka back in here and get the fuck out. I need relief."

"Good evening, papa."

I drop my cigarette on the ground without bothering to step on it. Maybe my father's right — it's time for him to retire. But how the fuck will I get an heir? I need help.

There's one person I can call on for assistance in these matters. I don't like involving the Greeks in Italian business, but... they're our cousins. She answers after a few rings and it sounds like she's at a nightclub. She has an inordinate amount of time for parties...

"Ciao?"

I can barely hear her over the sound of the music.

"Miss Pagonis. It's Van."

She giggles. "Duh. What's happening? You finally have work for me?"

"How soon can you come back to Italy?"

Single AF On The Amalfi Coast

JODI ROSE

I'm the last single woman in my family.

Three months in Italy, and I haven't had so much as a kiss, but my younger cousin Raven gets married to her college boyfriend and he looks like a dream. I drop a congratulatory comment on her photo, but my heart sinks.

You ugly, Jodi. Get used to it and stop chasing all these men out of your league. Settle with Kyle. He's the best you can do. Maybe mama was right. I'm not the marrying kind, anyway. I spent all my dating years focused on school and look at where that got me...

"Edo!"

The bartender gives me a sympathetic look. Ugh. Edo is so hot. Too bad all the hot guys are gay, especially in Italy, apparently.

"What happened?"

"Look at this."

I show him my phone and Edo cracks a smile. "Beautiful! Is she your sister?"

"No, my cousin. She's getting married and here I am... single... again."

And I'm running away from my problems with a one-way ticket to Italy. When my family finds out I'm not coming back, they're going to lose their minds. Everyone already thinks I'm crazy for leaving Kyle...

"Fuck your ex, Jodi. Seriously, fuck him," Edo says with all the passion of a best friend, even if we barely know each other.

I have major regrets about getting drunk my first night here and spilling all the drama about my ex-boyfriend to a bartender, but at least it made us fast friends. Although I'm not sure if Edo just likes the fact that Americans tip, unlike our Italian friends. He always has a way of scamming some extra euros out of me. At least he's a damn good listener.

I groan and dramatically lean against the bar as I make a proclamation that I wholeheartedly believe.

"I'm never going to get with another guy again. This is it. I'm dying alone."

I've read the statistics. Or at least I've read what women on Lipstick Alley say about the statistics. I'm a thick, well-educated black woman who is tired of the dusties and has real ass standards — according to the internet, I'm dying alone.

Edo grins and shakes his head. Since he learned I was American, he's done everything in my power to take me under his wing since I got here. I just hate getting too far out of my comfort zone, so I've ditched all his invitations to visit the local clubs in favor of spending my nights drinking cocktails alone and checking social media. I'm in Italy. I should have daily adventures and bread. I can't forget the delicious ass bread.

"You will not die alone," Edo says. "At least not without trying... my latest cocktail creation."

Edo does a dramatic dance before revealing some clear beverage that looks like some horrible mix of vodka, vermouth and orange juice.

Good. I want to get completely fucked up.

"That looks... clear."

"You'll love it, I promise."

"Will drinking really make the pain go away?" I muse, twirling the glass around so the little orange peel swirls inside it. Kyle. Why do you always miss the ones who fuck you up the most?

Hopefully, this drink will get my ain't shit ex off my mind, but let's be real. What I really need is a summer romance. Ha. Like that's going to happen in a country where half the people think I'm a prostitute because of my skin color.

"Yes. It will. Absolutely." Edo replies with a wink.

"Cheers." I swirl the drink around despite Edo's repeated claims I ruin his creations by doing that. I pour it down my throat and taste a pleasant citrus flavor before a powerful vodka burn. It takes everything in my power to get the rest of the drink down my throat. Whew! That was a damn burn.

"What the hell did you put in that?"

Edo winks, but offers no response. Tricky ass Italian.

"My shift ends in ten," he says. "I'll take you out tonight to Jalousie. No getting out of it this time to watch *Empire* in your apartment."

How the fuck does this skinny ass white boy know me so well already? I shake my head, prepared to reject his offer to take me to the club, but Edo won't let it go. He wriggles his brows suggestively.

He loves regaling me with stories about all the shenanigans that go down at the Amalfi Coast nightclubs. I'm not really a nightclub girl. Small bars like this one fit me better, but didn't I come to Italy to have fun? Meet someone? I should put in some effort.

The only men who give me any attention are the

creeps on the beach who say so much nasty shit to me in Italian that I'm glad I don't understand.

Maybe I'll meet better men at the club, especially a club with a fancy ass French name like this one. Jalousie. Wait... Edo's mentioned Jalousie to me before in the past.

"Ain't that the club with the mafia shootout you told me about?"

I don't believe half the shit that comes out of Edo's mouth, but he loves regaling me with stories about the real Italian mafia, which he claims is apparently far worse than any mafia in Long Island or Staten Island. How could anyone who lives in one of the most beautiful parts of the world hurt and kill other people? I think he likes telling tall tales to impress tourists.

I get people on Staten Island killing each other, but the Amalfi Coast? Hell fucking no. The sea is perfectly blue, the air smells fresh constantly, and it's plain peaceful out here. Italians have a rich culture, amazing food, better wine and the guys here are hot.

Not every guy, but when you walk down the streets here, you definitely encounter more than a few hotties. They all dress like supermodels, too. I've never seen so many regular ass people sporting Gucci and Fendi.

"Yes," Edo says. "But you're here for 9 more months, right? Have a fling. Don't tell him your real name... and disappear. You can find a hot and incredibly rich man to spoil you during your trip."

"Wait... is this a gay club or my type of club?"

Edo chuckles. "The guys are hot. I didn't say they were gay. You haven't earned your way into going to a gay club with me yet."

"Wow, Edo. I thought we had something going here."

Edo shrugs. "My private life is my private life. That's how it is in Italy. Your private life, on the other hand, is my playground. I'll introduce you to people. I know people who frequent Jalousie."

"Hot guys?"

"Eh..."

"Hot straight guys?" I correct myself before he answers. I don't want Edo tricking me into going out for nothing.

"Not exactly... I have a girl friend in town who goes all the time — Cassia Pagonis."

He says the name like I'm supposed to know who the fuck that is.

"Who the fuck is that?"

Edo chuckles. "A very fun girl with very hot brothers."

I perk up a little until Edo tells me they're all married. Great.

"Great. They're married..."

Before Edo can reassure me (again) more customers wander into the bar and Edo scurries to the other end of the bar to take orders.

I gaze into my phone again, looking at pictures from Raven's wedding. My cousin looks gorgeous, but I can't help a twisted pang of envy. I know it's wrong but... will that ever happen for me?

My homegirls from college keep sending me articles about the sorry state of marriage for black women. Alyssa says that we need to divest completely from marriage and just have fun.

My idea of fun isn't keeping a collection of all "my dicks" in a private folder on my phone. I want the real fucking thing! Even if the world loves reminding me that 'the real thing' only happens for white women or black women with the lightest dusting of melanin... I want to believe in love.

I scroll past Raven's pictures and my feed is all babies, new puppies, new jobs, new houses, new apartments, new husbands... new everything. Before Italy, I was just doing the same old shit. I wanted to shake things up. I don't know why my life hasn't transformed entirely. I'm in the prettiest place on earth — the Amalfi Coast.

Edo's shift ends, and he calls my name from the other end of the bar, beckoning me over to the cash register.

"Any tip for me today?"

"I saw you slip that five euro note out of my wallet. I think we're good."

Edo shrugs. "Sorry, this job doesn't pay well."

"I get it. I'll pay for our drinks tonight. Happy?"

"Incredibly."

I shouldn't be offering to pay for anyone's drinks, honestly, but I tell myself that I'll worry about all the damn money I'm spending once I get back to America. I have nine months of freedom and then I can worry about these damn bills and loans and everything else.

Edo drags me off my stool, and we step outside into the cobblestone street. I'll never get over how beautifully blue everything is here. The streets smell like the ocean, pastries, wine and cigarettes, of course. People sell jewelry and fruits on the streets and the Italian accents are... gorgeous. My Italian's still crap, despite Edo's best efforts to teach me a few phrases.

At least I don't have to hear all the street harassment thrown my way, which is plentiful. Edo replies defensively to a grey-haired man who calls something lewd in my direction and grabs me tighter. "Fuck these guys," he says. "You aren't that fat."

I swear, I'll never get used to how fucking blunt they are. But I appreciate Edo doing his best to defend me. We can hear the music from Jalousie echoing down the street before we get close.

"Isn't it early for the club?"

"Why are you so fucking American?" Edo asks, linking arms with me. "Relax."

"EDOARDO!" A shrill voice with a strange accent calls from across the street. I know Italian accents by now, at least how people from the Coast sound when speaking English, and this girl sounds different.

"That's Cass," Edo says to me, a smile breaking out across his handsome face. "Chin up. She'll love you."

Edo waves to the girl across the street and she struts over to us, sticking her hand out to stop the cars making their way down the cobblestone streets. They don't even honk as she passes.

The first thing I notice about her is how striking she is. She's tall, with curly dark brown hair pinned up out of her face and flowing down her back. She's wearing crazy high heels, like all the European girls do, a short leather skirt and a tight black leather crop top.

With her dark red lipstick, she looks like a film noir femme fatale... and she stares like one.

"Edo... is this your American friend?"

She turns to me and smiles. Shit, her accent might be strong, but her English is perfect. Cass's hair falls over her shoulders, her curls carrying a soft eucalyptus scent.

"Jodi Rose," I say, happy to have some female company around here, not like there's anything wrong with Edo. "Nice to meet you."

She takes my hand, three silver Cartier bracelets sliding down her wrist. Wow. Her bracelets aren't the only expensive item of clothing she has.

"Cass Pagonis. I'm sure Edo has told you all sorts of horrible stories about me."

"I did not!"

Edo definitely did. But Cass doesn't seem like a crazy party girl. She rolls her eyes and brushes him off.

"I'm here on the Coast working for my cousin's family," Cass says. "I'm from Thessaloniki. My idiot brothers want me back next week, unfortunately. But I could use a night out before I go."

Edo claps his hands. "Yay! Party time. Too bad Jalousie only caters to the most chauvinistic mafia pigs you can imagine."

"I thought you said they were hotties?!"

"They are," Edo says. "But they might be assholes."

Now he tells me. Edo would have said anything to get me out of my damn apartment. I hope I don't regret it.

"Watch it," Cass cautions, an impish smile on her face. "Those chauvinistic mafia pigs are my cousins and brothers."

Edo shrugs. "Fine. Fine. But I need dick too. Gay rights."

Cass swats his shoulder.

"Edo, why don't you let me take her for the night? There's no one at Jalousie for you, and you can go meet up with Klaus or... that other one."

Edo suddenly straightens his back and reminds both of us that just because he's gay doesn't mean he's given up on old world chivalry.

"I can't send Jodi off with a stranger," he says.

I appreciate the sentiment, but I don't know if Edo would do much damage against... any man who weighed more than his slight 108 lb frame.

"I'm fine," I tell him. "Seriously."

"I'm armed anyway," Cass says. I think she's joking, but neither of them laughs. Is she serious? She doesn't look armed, and she looks more like a model than someone who knows how to use a weapon.

I could use a female friend in my life over here. I've got plenty of female friends back home, but they all want to talk about Kyle and my "healing journey". They don't want to hear that I'm still lost after all these months.

Edo shrugs. "If you insist."

"I insist," I tell him. "You've done enough taking care of me. Plus, I'll get to know my new friend... Cass."

"Exactly," Cass says. "Jodi... I think we can become wonderful friends. We can swap stories about Edo."

"There are no stories about Edo," he chimes in. "Because Edo is an incredible friend and a better bartender."

"Shoo," Cass says. "I can handle things from here."

Edo doesn't quite walk off, but he checks his phone and begins texting furiously to plan his next move.

"It's the last time they have DJ Fat Camel playing here. We'll dance, drink and later, I'll take you home, yes?"

"That sounds good to me."

"Well, you have my number if Cass abandons you on the top of a Ferris wheel," Edo says as he swipes four times quickly across his screen and then shoves his phone into his pocket.

Cass rolls her eyes. "I have done nothing of the sort. Get out of here, you big drama queen."

"Ciao!"

Cass and I say "Ciao!"

Edo walks down the cobblestone streets and lights a cigarette before disappearing around the corner. Cass breathes a sigh of relief and turns to me.

"I just think you're perfect," she says.

Weird comment to make, but I mumble a gracious thank you, assuming something got lost in translation.

"Do you have friends with you?" Cass asks, taking out a hand mirror and fixing her bright red lipstick.

"No. I'm here solo tripping. Had a quarter life crisis and... here I am."

"Do you like Italy?" she asks genuinely. Her eyes are so intense.

"It's beautiful."

"Not as pretty as Greece," Cass says. "But I agree. Shall we go in?"

"We should head to the back of the line," I say, my stomach knotting as I see the line stretched around the block. I hope we can even get into the club.

Cass grins, unperturbed by the growing line outside Jalousie.

"My cousin owns the place. Come on, we go in through the back."

Before I can protest, she takes my hand and we walk around a back alley that smells like trash, vomit and again — cigarettes. Cass drags me over to a door and surveys me once before touching the handle.

"Very proper outfit. Excellent. Let's go. Ready to dance?"

I nod, even if I'm nervous. Sure, I'm trying to have an adventure tonight, but I just met this chick. How do I know she isn't crazy? Well, she has Edo's backing, so at least she'll be a good time. Edo definitely knows how to have fun if his clubbing stories are even 55% true.

Cass punches in a six-digit code and the back door to the club opens. I can smell the club before I hear the music and Cass drags me in through the back before I can second guess myself. What am I really doing? I don't know this chick at all and I agreed to go clubbing with her? Is Edo's word really enough?

Once we're in the back door, a man appears. He's

tall, with dark brown slicked back hair, tattoos all over his arms and grey eyes. He has broad shoulders, but is otherwise lean and very muscular. He's handsome, but it's too bad he smokes. I can smell the cigarettes from a distance.

"Cass? What the fuck are you doing here?" he asks, seeming genuinely upset.

"Shut the fuck up, Enzo," Cass snaps, her expression changing suddenly into a disapproving scowl. "I have business here."

The man smirks. He's around Cass' height, but he looks... greasy.

"Is that her?"

"Mind your fucking business."

Cass pushes him hard so we can get past him. The grey-eyed man's eyes land on me and he runs his hand over his jawline before snickering.

"He's going to kill you."

"Shut up," Cass snarls. Enzo laughs and raises his hands in defeat.

"Enjoy your night," he says to me in a sing-song voice. For the first time, I feel real hesitation. But Cass grabs my hand and drags me inside of the club.

Cass drags me all the way to the tables and chairs surrounding the dance floor, chatting excitedly and peppering me with questions about America. I struggle to understand her accent at first, but then I get into the rhythm of her voice and it's easier for us to communicate.

I have to listen in so hard that I barely scan the room we enter. At least the nightclub has a nice interior, and it doesn't seem like any ghetto shit might pop off. Another Edo exaggeration, it seems. I relax as Cass sets me up at a small, two-person table.

"I'll get you a drink. Wait here. If anyone comes to talk to you, tell them you are with Cass Pagonis. That will shut them up."

Before I can protest, or offer to come with her, Cass disappears. Shit. I guess I have to wait here. I already have five texts from Edo about the hotties he met at the club a few doors over. Damn, he moves quick. I've been here for weeks already and I still haven't met a heterosexual male who hasn't been an incredibly old and excessively horny man offering for me to be his 'African prostitute' — offers I have obviously declined.

Cass returns quickly, before I have any time to worry with two shots, each one with some blue flavoring at the bottom.

"Okay, Jodi. This is to a long and beautiful friendship between us, starting with one crazy night, yeah?"

I nod. "Hell yeah. I've never done anything like this before."

I blurt out the last part nervously, but Cass has a way of soothing me. She just smiles and nods. "Don't be scared! I'm a good Greek girl. Now come on... we'll take the shots together."

She counts us down.

"1... 2... 3..."

I take the shot — and it's the last thing I remember about that night.

Not An Italian Woman

VAN

"What the fuck? Cass!"

"I did what you asked. I have a girl in the back of the Escalade. I did an excellent job. She took the pills very well."

I slam the door shut. Cass must have given this girl elephant tranquilizers because she doesn't even fucking flinch.

"I gave you a list of characteristics, you Greek bitch."

"Careful, Van. Gal's in a boat a few miles off the coast. Don't make me call him on you."

"I said blonde. I said twenty-one. I said 5'4" tall, and I said thin. Does the woman in the back of this fucking Escalade look anything like I told you?"

My voice trembles with rage and that irritating

Greek cousin of mine just smiles and fishes a hand-rolled, loose cigarette from her skirt pocket.

"Do you have a lighter?"

"You sound bored. Don't you understand I could shoot you dead and drop your fucking body in the sea for this?" I growl.

Cass snickers. "You could try. Now, do you have a fucking lighter or not?"

I slam the lighter into my bratty cousin's outstretched palm. She lights her cigarette, that impish smile across her fucking face. Never trust a Greek bearing gifts. Why the fuck didn't I remember that before calling her? I only called the little brat because she likes money enough to keep my secret.

"What were you thinking?"

"Men don't know what they want," she says. "That's what I was thinking.'

"No! I know exactly what I want. I wanted a small, blond woman who belongs in the life, not a foreigner... not an African."

"Ignorant cunt," Cass snaps, slamming the heel of her boots into my calf. "She's African American. They're very cultured."

I want to break her in half. If she didn't have three of the most annoying brothers, perhaps I would.

"I don't want her."

"Too bad. She's what you get."

That little shit... Cass nonchalantly smokes. Doesn't she have a child now? That poor baker's son must be at home caring for her brat while she fucks with my life across the sea. If she didn't have a child, I would have at least attempted to smother her by now.

Instead, I'll give my bratty Greek cousin another chance to do the fucking job right.

"Go out again and find exactly what I asked for."

"You idiot. I drugged her and set her up for this. If she wakes up, she could go to the police, and this happens in your new nightclub? I'll be in Greece and your stupid club will be bankrupt. Does that sound wise?"

"Fuck, Cass. How could you fucking do this to me?"

"I didn't know you were so racist, Van."

"It's not racist. Fuck. I don't expect you to understand."

"Do you know any other words besides fuck? I'm leaving. I did what I came here to do. Sandros is waiting for me on the boat."

"I'm never hiring you again."

"You always say that. Why don't you trust me, cousin?"

"Because you're an evil Greek bitch. That's why."

Cass laughs like I paid her a compliment.

"That's going to be my next tattoo. Her name is Jodi, by the way. She seems very nice. I think she has a good curvy shape too. But what do I know? Ciao, Van."

She leans forward and kisses me on the cheek, leaving the red print of her lipstick behind. I rub my forehead as she walks off. Fuck. I've made a huge mistake and now I have a drugged woman in the back of my fucking car.

I call Enzo. Because he's the brother you call when you have a drugged woman in the back of your car and you need to go kill a Jew.

"What do you want?"

"Meet me at the beach."

"What part?" Enzo huffs. He wants to know if this is for a murder or a party. He'll know by my answer.

"Southern shore. I have a problem."

"Killing David tonight?"

My jawline clenches. "Yes. But I have another problem. I can't do this alone."

"Can't you get Eddie to do it?"

"No. I need you..."

Enzo can be a lazy fuck sometimes.

"See you in ten."

"Be there in seven."

Fuck. I get into the car and glance behind me at the woman laid across the leather seats of my Escalade. Jodi. I've never seen a woman like her in my life. She's confusing, and she's definitely not what I wanted. I need a woman I can produce an heir with—a surrogate to give me a child and then disappear. What the hell was Cass thinking disobeying me?

She's more proof we need to tighten the hold on our family. Nobody respects the Doukas name anymore.

She's still asleep when I get to the beach. I peer into the back seat at her chest rising and falling. At least she isn't dead. I don't have the stomach to dispose of two bodies tonight. Enzo rolls his car next to mine, rolling down the window and expelling an enormous cloud of marijuana smoke.

"You showed up high?"

"Relax. I also brought Eddie."

"Ciao, Uncle Van."

"Why the fuck did you bring Eddie?"

"Didn't you bring someone?" Enzo smirks, which means he probably noticed Cass at the club earlier and pieced everything together. She's still in the back of the Escalade and I don't need my fucking brother or my idiot nephew involved with this.

The last thing I need is Enzo dragging out my personal business for his habitual mockery.

"Shut up. Where's David tonight?"

"Gambling. As usual. Does Ana know we're doing this?"

My brother irks me sometimes. "Do you think Ana fucking knows?"

"Why so upset, brother? Working with the Greek cunt didn't work out? Who could have predicted that..."

"Shut up, Enzo."

Eddie glances up from his phone for the first time.

"Either of you have a cigarette?"

"You're too young to smoke," Enzo says.

"Fuck off. You're only three years older than me," Eddie protests, throwing a powerful punch on Enzo's shoulder. My brother doesn't flinch.

"Doesn't matter. He's your superior. You listen to him," I growl. If papa had taught them discipline from the beginning, neither of them would be like this. Now it's my responsibility whenever we go out to remind these fucks what *cosa nostra* is really all about. Our way of life is falling apart.

Eddie shrugs, and Enzo hands our nephew a cigarette, giving me a knowing look. After what we do tonight, he'll need more than a cigarette. We both remember our first kill and it wasn't pretty.

After two puffs, Eddie grins. "Are we working or what? I have more cunts to catch tonight."

"Quiet, Eddie," Enzo grumbles, tapping away on his phone. "Okay. I've got him. He's five blocks away."

I wonder what weapons my brother and nephew brought tonight. We'll need more than my pistol.

"Who is he drinking with tonight?" I grunt. How many motherfuckers will we have to take out?

Enzo shakes his head. "You won't like this."

"Five other men from his family. We can't be sure he'll leave the place alone."

"We need someone to lure him out," Eddie suggests. "A prostitute. Or a woman who can act like one. I'll get my girlfriend."

"You're still seeing Zara?"

I told Eddie to leave Zara alone after the last incident. I don't want to deal with another domestic problem.

"Why should I stop? She always takes me back."

"At least she makes a believable prostitute," Enzo says, shrugging. Eddie laughs, not even bothering to defend the woman he claims to love. Yes, she's a foreigner, but that shouldn't matter if he's chosen her. Love. This is what papa wants me to fight so hard for? Whatever he has for this family isn't love, and I have no intention of repeating his mistakes. I'll leave love for the younger generation, although Eddie doesn't leave me with much hope.

"Show some respect," I growl. "We're not using Zara."

Eddie puffs out his chest, but he's careful not to push me too hard. I'm just as likely to put out a hit on him as anyone else.

"Why not? She's mine to use," he says defiantly until I raise my eyebrow and silence my nephew.

Unfortunately, my idiot brother speaks up in Eddie's favor.

"We don't have a choice," Enzo says. "Unless you have someone else for us to use?"

The smirk on his irritating fucking face tells me he knows exactly who and what he's asking for. Bastard.

He knows what Cass did for me. Either that, or he suspects. My face betrays nothing. Unlike my father and Matteo, I don't let Lorenzo get under my skin.

"I have nothing for you."

"Except the unconscious immigrant in the back of your car," Enzo replies calmly, stealing another cigarette from Eddie's shirt pocket. All they fucking do is smoke and run women. Maybe my father's right and I need to take control of this family. My stomach lurches at that thought, combined with the knowledge of the woman in the backseat of my car.

"Why bother drugging and kidnapping a prostitute if we can't even use her?"

"If he doesn't want her, I'll have her," Eddie snickers, taking the lit cigarette from Enzo and taking a huge puff.

"Put out the fucking cigarette. We don't need a lure, we need patience, something you stupid fucks know nothing about. We drive to the Jew and we wait for him to exit alone. We trust he will exit alone. If we can't get him tonight, we get him tomorrow night. Understood?"

My tone sets them straight this time. Enzo puts out the cigarette. They can't disobey direct orders. Even if they might not fear me, they both fear papa. Then again, judging by Eddie's averted eyes and sheepish glances, perhaps I'm more terrifying than I thought. Matteo would have whipped them into shape. I hope Albania is worth it, you stupid fuck.

The boys get into Enzo's car and he drives away first. I want to take my time out here on this beach, with this woman, and assess this mess of a fucking situation. Never trust a Greek bearing gifts. How many fucking times has papa warned me about the Pagonis family? They're tricksters. I wipe my sweaty hands on black jeans and open the back of the car.

Fuck you, Cass.

She couldn't have made a bigger effort to deviate from my exact specifications for what I wanted in a woman — and, more importantly, what I wanted in a womb. How am I supposed to produce an heir with... her? I specifically said blonde. This woman couldn't possibly come anywhere close to blonde. And her skin color...

My stomach twists in an incomprehensible knot as I stare at her unconscious body, a tight party dress barely covering her thick thighs. Her thighs are... large. Everything about her is larger than the typical Amalfi Coast club girl. She doesn't look like she's afraid to eat anything denser than lettuce, to start. She has curves. Very full curves. She's not my type, but my cock doesn't appear to get the message. I feel like a fucking teenager.

She isn't suitable for this job, but perhaps she'll have her uses. I'll examine my prize later. I have to kill the Jew before the woman wakes up. Considering how little Cass obeyed my instructions, I may not have much time. I follow Enzo's route to the bar where the Jews hang around, shooting dice and drinking like the rest of us. I have nothing against the religion — it's the people. It's tradition.

Our families have been at war for generations. They blame the past on our people, even if two generations ago, they were the ones bankrupting humble Italian families and taking ears and noses as collateral for unpayable loans. Without the family, without the protection and organization under papa and his trusted advisors, they would have owned all of us, kept us no better than slaves.

So no, I don't hate the Jews — but I have pride in myself and my family. I am an Italian man. Nobody owns me.

Enzo texts me when he's in position. This is the boring part. I stop the car and allow everything to settle into pure silence — except for a soft sound in the back seat. Snoring. I find the sound unsettling. I spend nearly every waking moment that I can alone, so her soft noises remind me that there's a stranger, another fucking problem, lying in my back seat.

The crowd around the Jewish bar thins shortly after our arrival. It's late enough that couples and foreigners and groups of students on vacation spill out of the bar and onto the cobblestone streets. Foreigners don't care who owns which bar or which club. They just want to spend their money, blissfully unaware of the work that goes into keeping Italy their playground.

I know the man I'm going to kill. We're friendly. In public, us Italians hold nothing against the Jews and they hold nothing against us. Our war happens in secret. I attended school with David. We played football together in high school. Tonight, I'll chop him up into several pieces and... well, you'll see how it goes.

After an hour, Enzo finally messages me. Eddie saw him and he's leaving through the back, drunk and stumbling home alone. Eddie has eyes on him, but we'll need to move the cars to get him. Easy. I command Enzo to pick him up since he has Eddie on the street. We'll take him to the beach. It's the best place for a born and raised Italian to die.

We drive thirty miles up the coast to the beach where we work. You don't shit where you eat, right? The woman sleeps peacefully in the back seat the entire time. It's for the best. Enzo and Eddie wait for me to get there, only pulling the Jew out when I leave my car. They might be fuckups, but when it's important, they make an effort at obedience.

He doesn't struggle and not just because of the gun Eddie presses into his stomach. He knows his time has come. Everyone in the life knows this is most likely how we're going to die, a bullet to the fucking head that's had our name on it for years.

"Take his hood off. He knows who we are."

Enzo obeys, but Eddie keeps a tight grip on the Jew before removing the cloth hood from the man's head. He raises his gaze instantly.

"I don't want to do this," I tell him.

"Don't give me the speech, Van," David chokes out. "Just finish it. Don't draw it out."

"You know what you've done and why this is happening. We have to send a message."

"I have money, Van. Enough money to set the three of you fucks free. You could leave Italy. Forever. Money. Information. I have anything you want."

Every man behaves differently when he faces death. Death isn't pretty. You piss and shit yourself in front of other men. You cry for your mother. You deny what's happening — and with the Jew, you attempt to strike a bargain. You attempt to give your killer what he wants, hoping he sets you free and allows you to disappear. Believe me, you get this far and free yourself, you want to disappear.

The Jew has made a grave miscalculation. I will never and would never choose money over family. Even if it's just my sister Ana, who I strongly dislike.

"We don't need money from you people anymore."

"I know. I know... But Van... we have history."

"Fuck, I'm tired of this. Uncle, can I shoot him?"

"Eddie, no. That's not how we do things."

Enzo puts his hand on the man's shoulders and nods. "Yes," he says. "We give them time to pray to their God and whisper any last words before we gut them and stuff their dicks in their mouth."

Now the man takes a piss. I swear I could fucking kill Enzo for scaring him. That's the last thing we need.

"I promise we won't desecrate your corpse. Now pray if you must."

"I have a request," David pleads.

"Hm?"

I don't like the idea of a dying man making requests, but considering Enzo just pushed him to the edge of fear, I feel a touch generous. Just a touch.

"My chain. Give it to my daughter. Please. That's all I ask. I want her to know that I was thinking about her."

"Your daughter is three. She won't remember you," Enzo says. Fucking hell, I want to kill my brother.

"Don't listen to him. Eddie, take the chain. We'll do what the man says."

"Take my gun off him?"

"He won't run," I say to him, but of course, I

can't exactly make these assurances. It's just a guess. He's alone with three armed mafiosos on the beach. He would have to be an idiot to run. I make a very incorrect judgment about our captive's intelligence. As Eddie lowers his gun and begins removing the man's star hanging around his neck, he shoves his elbow into Eddie's side and throws a hard kick toward Enzo before taking off down the beach.

Stupid fuck... I take off after him, pulling out my gun as I run. The poor bastard isn't quick — something I would have considered in his position. He played football with me. He should know who he's dealing with. I throw my leg out and catapult the Jew to the sand. He cries out as his body goes flying. Enzo and Eddie catch up with me as I trip and roll over, holding my gun aloft. I can't stop what they're about to do now. The Jew made a mistake by running.

Enzo throws a hard kick into the man's side. Eddie laughs as blood spurts from the man's face. They beat him for a while until he can't make any other sound except a whimper and a prayer. When he prays, I stop them with my hand.

"Before you die, we'll be needing that information you promised?"

He looks up at us as if he won't say anything. Then I watch the defeat flow from his face. Information. He'll give it up to us. The Jews have strong bonds, but not as strong as ours. They don't kill the way we do, so their people don't fear giving up information. At least I can justify this to myself.

I killed a man for information sits better with my conscience than killing a man for Ana. If I don't follow orders, I'll be the one kneeling on the beach next. I can't have that happen.

This isn't exactly going in the order I planned it, but I still need that information. The man gazes up at us, blood in his mouth, his eyes glued shut and swollen. He's already half dead.

"What do you need to know?"

Enzo whispers the question in quiet Italian. The man shakes his head.

"You're messing with the wrong people."

"Thanks for the advice," Enzo says. Before I give the order, he empties his gun. Two in the man's head and one in his chest. My stomach tightens. Even Eddie's eyes spark open, stunned. The worst part of all happens after the gunshots — a loud, blood-curdling scream. The three of us turn around to see her standing there, wide-awake and screaming her head off like a banshee.

My woman...

Fuck.

Click here to order Forced To Surrogate:
https://linktr.ee/JamilaJasper

Sign up to get a text message notification when my next book drops: https://slkt.io/gxzM

Extremely Important Links

ALL BOOKS BY JAMILA JASPER
https://linktr.ee/JamilaJasper
SIGN UP FOR EMAIL UPDATES
Bit.ly/jamilajasperromance
SOCIAL MEDIA LINKS
https://www.jamilajasperromance.com/
GET MERCH
https://www.redbubble.com/people/
jamilajasper/shop
GET FREEBIE (VIA TEXT)
https://slkt.io/qMk8
READ SERIAL (NEW CHAPTERS WEEKLY)
www.patreon.com/jamilajasper

JAMILA JASPER

Diverse Romance For Black Women

More Jamila Jasper Romance

Pick your poison...

Delicious interracial romance novels for all tastes. Long novels, short stories, audiobooks and more.

Hit the link to experience my full catalog.

FULL CATALOG BY JAMILA JASPER:

https://linktr.ee/JamilaJasper

Patreon

12+ SEASONS OF BWWM ROMANCE SERIAL CHAPTERS

🔥 NEW RELEASE 🔥

Powerless: Dark Bully BWWM Romance

Read the ongoing story POWERLESS and ALL the previous releases for a small monthly cost.

Instantly access all six seasons of *Unfuckable* (Ben & Libby's story) with 375 chapters.

For a small monthly fee, you get exclusive access to my all this & my recently completed serial Despicable (275 chapters)

www.patreon.com/jamilajasper

PATREON HAS MORE THAN THE ONGOING SERIAL AND PREVIOUS SERIAL RELEASES...

⚡ INSTANT ACCESS ⚡

- NEW merchandise tiers with **t-shirts, totes, mugs,** stickers and MORE!
- **FREE paperback** with all new tiers
- **FREE short story audiobooks** and audiobook samples when they're ready
- #FirstDraftLeaks of Prologues and first chapters **weeks** before I hit publish
- Behind the scenes notes
- Polls and story contribution
- Comments & LIVELY community discussion with likeminded interracial romance readers.

LEARN MORE ABOUT SUPPORTING A
DIVERSE ROMANCE AUTHOR

www.patreon.com/jamilajasper

Thank You Kindly

Thank you to all my readers, new and old for your support with this new year.

I look forward to making 2022 an INCREDIBLE year for interracial romance novels. I want to thank you all for joining along on the journey.

Thank you to my most supportive readers:
Christine, Trinity, Monica, Juliette, Letetia, Margaret, Dash, Maxine, Sheron, Javonda, Pearl, Kiana, Shyan, Jacklyn, Amy, Julia, Colleen, Natasha, Yvonne, Brittany, June, Ashleigh, Nene, Nene, Deborah, Nikki, DeShaunda, Latoya, Shelite, Arlene, Judith, Mary, Shanida, Rachel, Damzel, Ahnjala, Kenya, Momo, BJ, Akeshia, Melissa, Tiffany, Sherbear, Nini, Curtresa, Regina, Ashley, Mia, Sydney, Sharon, Charlotte, Assiatu, Regina, Romanda, Catherine, Gaynor, BF, Tasha, Henri, Sara, skkent, Rosalyn, Danielle, Deborah, Kirsten, Ana, Taylor, Charlene Louanna, Michelle, Tamika,

Lauren, RoHyde, Natasha, Shekynah, Cassie, Dreama, Nick, Gennifer, Rayna, Jaleda, Anton, Kimvodkna, Jatonn, Anoushka, Audrey, Valeria, Courtney, Donna, Jenetha, Ayana, Kristy, FreyaJo, Grace, Kisha, Stephanie E., Amber, Denice, Marty, LaKisha, Latoya, Natasha, Monifa, Alisa, Daveena, Desiree, Gerry, Kimberly, Stephanie M., Tarah, Yolanda, Kristy, Gary, Janet, Kathy, Phyllis, Susan

Join the Patreon Community.
www.patreon.com/jamilajasper